CT KLASS

Cease Upon the Midnight

First published by Du Y Moroedd Publishing 2026

First edition

ISBN: 978-1-9194270-0-3

This book was professionally typeset on Reedsy.
Find out more at reedsy.com

For everyone who doesn't know they are magic.

Especially Siân.

Chapter 1

April, 2003

The wolf's shadow moved again. Ziggy blinked, heart thudding, but it was only the shifting light from outside the window. The rain drummed on the caravan roof, drowning the faint music from the stereo beside her.

This wasn't the type of rock music that was meant to be played quietly, but the stereo's volume control was faulty. It either played too softly or too loudly. That's why Peter had given it to her in the first place. She didn't mind though; it was soothing.

Perched on a rickety stool from her father's old office, she rinsed her paintbrush in a chipped yellow mug of painty water. The caravan was cluttered with art supplies. Paper and pencils, ink stains and rags, chewed up rubbers and squeezed-to-death paint tubes were scattered around on every available surface. A few more old mugs sat nearby, some with half-finished cups of tea or lemonade in them. One bore the *Cadbury's Creme Egg* logo. Another featured a picture of an overstocked bookshelf and the slogan *I Have No Shelf Control.* She had to be careful not to wash her brush in cold tea by mistake. She'd done that more than once.

Ziggy yawned as she dipped her paintbrush into a blob of *Burnt Ochre*, blinking a few times at the canvas before adding a speck of the colour *just so*.

She scrunched up her nose, dropped her hand again and stood. Backing away from the painting, she eyed it dubiously. It wasn't meant to be acrylic. Ziggy had planned an ink drawing, but Miss Tucker had gently insisted that her idea of a twilit forest scene would be more atmospheric in living colour. Miss Tucker insisted a lot of things.

The deep greens and rich browns of the forest floor were lush and felt truly organic, while the shadows spoke ominously of menacing creatures, just out of sight. In the foreground, a sinewy, coal-black wolf lifted its muzzle and bared its fangs. A moon of *Titan Buff* and *Yellow Oxide*, tinged with *Vermillion Red* shone down on it.

There was a space on the right side of the canvas, in a gap she had left between the trees, ready to add the injured deer that she had been practicing sketching for weeks but had yet to perfect.

The rain had stopped, but the trees still dripped an irregular rhythm on the roof while Ziggy gazed at the canvas, paintbrush at her side.

She had been staring at it for so long that her eyes were stinging. The shapes before her no longer had any meaning. There were brushstrokes that she couldn't make sense of; some that she couldn't remember applying, the implied movement, just beyond the line of sight.

The late afternoon light shifted through the window across the canvas. The wolf's shadow seemed to move with it. Ziggy tilted her head, concentrating, listening intently, like the painting might growl.

A twig cracked loudly outside the door. She flinched. Her mother had walked down the garden to remind her it was time to go.

"Just a second, I'm nearly done," she called out.

She looked down at her hand, realising she'd got paint on her fingers. In her surprise, she'd touched her new dress with the brush. Swearing under her breath, she went to the sink to wash her hands, tried to sponge the brownish-orange stain from the hem of her dress, but it wouldn't come off with just water.

"I'm coming now," she said out loud, expecting the door to open at any moment. When it didn't, she went and opened it herself, looking out into the wet, overgrown garden. The trees and shrubs, heavy with late spring leaves and bright blossoms, glistened in the afternoon light. The clouds had cleared, but the earlier downpour had left the garden dripping and smelling earthy.

Just out of sight on the other side of the stone wall at the bottom of the garden was the churchyard, wrapped around with trees as tall as the church itself which cast perpetual damp shadows across the surrounding gardens.

There was no one around, not even Puck, though she made quiet "pspsps" sounds, hoping the little silver tabby was lurking in the moss nearby.

A cool breeze caught Ziggy's dark hair about her face and whipped a few loose pages off the table behind her, but there was no sign of the cat, or her mother, or any other living soul in the garden.

Somewhere in the distance, she heard a train whistle, deep and long like the call of a hunter's horn. She shivered, brushing away the childish thought, and closed the door again to finish tidying up.

But midway through sweeping handfuls of cornflakey sharpenings off the desk, seized by a whim, Ziggy picked up the nearest pencil and turned back to her painting. She traced the outline of a new figure in the space where she'd planned to put the deer.

In her mind's eye, she couldn't quite see yet what this figure was supposed to be. Not the deer, for sure. It was vaguely human at least, or perhaps one of those monstrous creatures, like the ones she always used to draw.

Miss Tucker had encouraged her away from fantasy art, explaining that she needed to explore other styles and subjects in order to succeed in her exams, and she had tried. She drew portraits, animals, still life and landscapes. She painted with acrylics, watercolours and oils. Her best work, though, was always when she let her hand move of its own accord, and inevitably, it created something beautiful and hideous and magical.

"Justine! Are you ready to go?"

Her mother's voice, above the sound of the raindrops and the stereo.

The shape on the canvas was still unclear. She didn't know what the figure running from the beast was, only that it was familiar. At least now she had an idea now of where this painting was going. She smiled as she put down the brush and switched off the stereo. Heading out into the cool damp air, she locked the door behind her, leaving the window open just a crack, so that Puck could find her way in when the rain started again.

Chapter 2

Algae fogged the aquarium glass. Ziggy stared at it, a furrow between her eyebrows, listening to the soft burble of the air pump.

"Mam, you need to let Megan sort your tablets for you. That's what those little boxes with the days of the week on are for."

"I can still count, Gary."

"I know you can, but those little tablets are fiddly, aren't they? You don't want to get in a mess again. Here's your cuppa."

Gary Briggs put the cup down on his mother's good left side, then sat down on the tired floral sofa next to his daughter.

Since the stroke, Peg's vision had been fading, and she needed a frame to move around. The little bungalow was as neat as ever. The family saw to that. Although clean, the sofa was worn, the carpet threadbare. Gary had offered to replace them, but Peg insisted there was no point. Grinning wickedly, she'd told him she wouldn't be around much longer to enjoy plush carpets and would rather spend her money making her family happy while she still could. Ziggy, who visited most days after school and every weekend, did not like to think about things like that.

"Where's the magnet, Nana?" she asked.

"The what?"

"The magnet cleaner. For the glass."

"It's there somewhere, Poppet," Nana Peg waved a dismissive hand, then dipped a custard cream into her tea on the little wooden table next to her armchair. "Have a biscuit, June."

"I'm alright, thanks," June Briggs replied with a weak smile. She looked pale, and Peg raised a knowing eyebrow, about to press, but June cut her off. "Justine, what are you doing?"

"Looking for the magnet, I want to clean the glass."

Rifling through the drawers in the cabinet under the aquarium, Ziggy tuned out as her parents chatted to Nana Peg about Megan, the young carer who came in to help her five mornings a week.

Underneath a flower press, a book on Celtic Mythology and a few loose sheets of art paper, Ziggy found what she was looking for. The other half of it was lying at the bottom corner of the tank collecting green slime, and she reconnected the two sides through the glass with a satisfying clunk, before gliding the chunk of plastic methodically up and down along the scummy sides of the aquarium. A clear trail followed in its wake, and Ziggy smiled contentedly.

"Yes, well, you know I think Megan's worth her weight in gold, but I'm still perfectly capable," Peg was complaining. "Besides, why are we still talking about me on Justine's birthday? Do you have any special plans, Poppet?"

"Hmm?"

"What are you doing for your birthday? Going out with your friends? Aren't you the last one to turn eighteen?"

Ziggy just shook her head, causing her mother to give a little annoyed huff.

"We're going out for a meal this evening, Peter's meeting us," she said.

"That's nice of him to drive down."

"Any excuse for a steak," said Gary, brushing biscuit crumbs from his salt and pepper beard.

Ziggy felt their eyes on the back of her head as she knelt on the floor. It made her itch. She dragged the magnet back and forth across the aquarium glass again.

"I can't say I'm not glad she doesn't have any interest in going out and getting drunk for her eighteenth," her father chuckled. "You're the only teenager I know who doesn't have *Toxic* set as a ringtone."

"Lena Meyer had an enormous party last month," said June. "Her parents booked out the rugby club, with food and a DJ. Justine didn't fancy it, but Eleanor next door went. She didn't get home until almost two in the morning."

"Lovely Lena," said Peg, over a slurp of tea. "Popular girl. I expect it was a bit rowdy, eh? Anyhow, that should have been a party for two, shouldn't it?"

"Yes, I think that's how Frank and Babs saw it," June agreed. "As far as the cost, I mean. They've indulged her a bit, since losing Nicky."

"What about that Jamie Cleary?" asked Peg. "Hasn't he got handsome all of a sudden? He came around to do my grass the other week and I thought it was his father, the bugger."

"His birthday isn't until July," said Ziggy without turning around, though she had finished cleaning the glass. "He's going to Alton Towers."

"You could have done something like that, if you wanted," her mother intoned gently. Ziggy lifted her shoulders and came back to sit on the sofa. She nibbled at the corner of a custard cream.

"That dress is a lovely colour on you."

"We picked it out special," said June. She was smiling, but there was the barest hint of sadness in her grey eyes.

"I got paint on it already," Ziggy said, tugging at the hem. It didn't feel like her birthday. It felt like a scene she was supposed to show up for.

"Of course you did," replied Peg warmly. "Now then. I know I wasn't supposed to get you a present but go have a look on the sideboard over there."

"Nana," Ziggy said, half-scolding.

"It didn't cost me a penny. Go on."

She went over to the polished oak sideboard and picked up the palm-sized black box with a little green adhesive ribbon stuck absurdly on top. Nana Peg's arthritic fingers wouldn't wrap a gift anymore, which Ziggy was glad for. She felt awkward enough opening things in front of people.

"Bring it here then. You know what it is. I always said you'd have it."

Taking the box over to Peg's chair, she carefully flipped it open without surprise to see the silver locket inside.

It was oval, about the size of a twenty-pence piece and delicately engraved with leaves, on a long, fine chain. Hinged on one side, it gleamed between her fingers as she opened it, not a speck of tarnish on its smooth sides. Inside was a tiny portrait of a solemn little girl in a forest-green dress, tilting her head curiously at the camera. Ziggy herself at around four years old.

"My pretty little Poppet," said Peg with a sigh. "I can't see her in there anymore, so you may as well have her to remind you what an extraordinary girl you are." She reached over and put a bony hand on top of her granddaughter's paint-stained one. "I know you have a hard time remembering that sometimes."

Ziggy looked into Peg's rheumy eyes, as blue as her own, and felt a sharp pang of grief. She understood why her grandmother was giving her the locket. The same reason she had paid for the caravan in the garden for her to use as an art studio when she started her A-Level course last year. The same reason she paid the deposit on Peter's flat. The hand on top of hers felt cool and dry, but it trembled.

"Thank you, Nana ."

* * *

Later, with the rain ticking again on the caravan roof in time to the rhythm of *The Foo Fighters*, Ziggy stood in front of her painting, leaning close. The locket lay open beside her. Two table lamps cast warm beams over the canvas, as well as the dusty overhead dome on the ceiling of the caravan, but she still had to squint at the pale, ghoulish figure that escaped through the trees, pursued by the wolf.

The black voids of its eyes were empty, but not blind. It struck her as more sorrowful than frightening. The sense of déjà vu it gave her was strong, and she smiled fondly as she added a touch of shadow at its feet.

It was full-dark out in the garden. She might sleep out here tonight. Puck already was , curled up, purring next to the stereo, her whiskers twitching in time to the music. Just as Ziggy reached out a hand to stroke her, the speakers crackled with a strange, stuttering buzz, startling Puck awake.

"How many times, Pucky? It's only a message."

Sure enough, a second later, Ziggy's Nokia lit up and bleeped.

She ignored it, reaching to adjust the stereo volume, turning it up only slightly, but causing the sound to jump much higher. Offended by the sudden cacophony, Puck leapt down and began weaving between her ankles, chirruping, and Ziggy crouched to scratch her behind the ears.

The music was too loud now, but thinking was worse. That's when the monsters came. Music helped. She sang along to the rock song on the stereo and painted until the song ended. Then another started. And another.

Chapter 3

"It's lunchtime, Justine."

"I know."

Miss Tucker stood watching her for a few moments. "That means it's time for you to leave," she said.

"I know. I'm done."

She spent another minute finishing her shading before she closed her sketchbook and put her pens away.

"Let me guess. You're going to eat a sandwich in the sixth form lounge and carry on drawing?" the teacher chuckled.

"Yeah," she admitted.

"I saw Felicity waiting for you, but you took so long I think she gave up..."

"I don't mind."

But Miss Tucker hesitated. She flipped open the cover of Ziggy's sketchbook again, regarding the front page thoughtfully. A coloured ink drawing of a tree, thick with summer leaves so lush they were almost fragrant on the page. The book was nearly full by now; she added to it every week.

"I spoke to your mum on the phone the other day... she's worried about your interview..."

Ziggy closed the sketchbook again and gathered it up into her bag with a roll of her eyes.

"Bit late for that."

"So... it didn't go well? You never really said-"

"It didn't."

She hefted her bag onto her shoulder, her face a mask of indifference, eyes on the floor.

"They must have been impressed by your portfolio..."

"Yeah, but I'm no good at talking to people."

"We went over everything they were likely to ask. Did they throw you an unexpected question?"

These were unexpected questions. Ziggy squirmed.

"I just froze up," she said.

Miss Tucker nodded. She had been a young, inexperienced teacher, fresh out of university, when Ziggy first met her six years ago, and sometimes Ziggy got the feeling that Miss Tucker hardly knew much more than she did. She found it hard to take the art teacher seriously at times, even with the neat bob and smart jackets Miss Tucker had taken to wearing lately.

"Your work speaks for itself, Justine," she said kindly. "That's what I told your mum. I'm sure you'll get an offer for September... I'm more worried about how things might go for you next year... socially."

"You said that in year eleven too," Ziggy shrugged. "And here I am. I'm fine."

"I know you are. I'm not trying to patronise you. It's not like in year seven when those boys used to kick footballs at you. But Justine- Ziggy-" her eyes snapped up at the use of the nickname. "How can you expect to start a new life, move away from home by yourself, when you still need reminding to eat your lunch... when you let all your friends go off and have birthday parties without you?"

Ziggy folded her arms, a shield against the ambush.

"Since when is having friends a criteria for success?"

"It's not, but-"

"I appreciate what you're trying to say though," she blurted defensively. "I'll try to make more effort with people if you think it'll help me in the long run."

"I do," said Miss Tucker gently, furrowing her brow. "You can't make it through life all by yourself."

Ziggy just nodded awkwardly. She left the art room, silently vowing to keep better track of time at the end of lessons in future, if nothing else then at least to avoid these sorts of conversations.

On her way down to the sixth form lounge, through corridors that were already empty, she stopped at her locker to collect her lunch. Felicity was at her own locker a few doors down, her boyfriend, Darren, waiting at the door to the hallway for her, puppylike. She looked over at him and then took her time closing her locker. The only Chinese-British pupil in an overwhelmingly bland and white school- at least that Ziggy knew of- Felicity radiated the kind of effortless confidence Ziggy could only wish for. She was gorgeous, clever and friendly; and could do miles better than this lanky nerd, but apparently, she thought he was cute, with the added bonus that he'd wait all day if she told him to.

"Coming to lunch?" she asked brightly.

Ziggy thought about her promise to Miss Tucker. She'd already made up her mind to eat in the relative peace and quiet of the lounge and wasn't braced to face the dining hall today. Perhaps tomorrow. She shook her head but smiled gratefully. Felicity smiled back and finally closed her locker, then went over to take the hand of the besotted boy waiting by the door.

Ziggy watched her go and plugged her earphones into her Walkman. Walking back up the corridor, she pushed open the door of the blessedly deserted sixth form lounge, commandeering her favourite low table at the back near the window where the light was good.

There were tables for studying and desks with computers on the other side of the room, but this corner was meant to be more social and comfy. The battered chairs were upholstered in green twill, and there were even a few cushions dotted about. Ziggy liked to sit on the floor, take off her shoes and crouch over the table to draw. Inevitably, someone would come along and sit on this side to drink their coffee or gossip, but she wouldn't speak to them, and they barely seemed to notice her. Sometimes, while she sat there alone, but surrounded by people, it seemed like she was a ghost haunting her own life.

Her music was blasting loudly in her ears, but even so, Ziggy couldn't help but notice when Motormouth Luke Chambers came barging into the lounge, slamming against the wall, and roaring with laughter. She glanced up from her drawing. Luke was wearing a black hoodie pulled up to cover his sandy hair; a good thing, considering the state of his companion, whose white shirt was stuck to his shoulders from the rain. Jamie Cleary took off his glasses, intending to wipe the drips from them but failed to find an article of clothing dry enough to be fit for purpose.

Miss Hunter; bleach-blonde, bottle-tanned, and infamous for her shrill rants, followed the boys in. Ziggy couldn't hear exactly what she said to them, but gathered it was about running in the corridor, and watched Luke's failed attempt to train his expression into something suitably sheepish. Jamie just blinked idiotically and nodded at whatever the teacher said before she marched back out. Luke started laughing again.

Ziggy removed one earphone just in time to hear him mutter the students' favourite, foul-mouthed nickname for the teacher.

"There's tissues over there," she said.

"Jesus!" Luke exclaimed, laying it on thick. "Where did you spring from?"

"Outer space," she replied.

Jamie just nodded his thanks at her and went to pull a couple of tissues from the box on the other table, using them to dry his glasses and face. He caught her eye with a familiar smile. She would have looked away from most people, but not him. Not Jamie. Not even now.

"I texted you on the weekend," he said.

"Did you?"

"Yeah. Just to say happy birthday."

"Oh… Thanks… Sorry."

He shrugged.

Ziggy wondered what that meant. Was it a *"Don't worry about it"* shrug, a *"What are you sorry for?"* shrug, or a passive aggressive *"Well, that's the last time I bother texting you"* shrug?

She put her earphone back in and turned back to her drawing but kept the volume lower now. She really was sorry not to have answered his text.

"You seriously need to get contact lenses sorted," Luke was saying. "I swear you're getting worse; you didn't even see Miss Hunter until you ran into her. How is it you're so good in the swimming pool though? Do you even *know* when to stop?"

"When I hit something," Jamie deadpanned. "I'm not as bad as I used to be, remember that time I broke my glasses on a school trip?"

"The saddest little mole bastard," Luke chortled. "They should've given Ziggy a fluorescent harness and a handful of Bonios at the end of the tour."

There was chatter in the hallway outside, getting steadily louder. Ziggy could still feel Jamie's eyes on her, and she knew he was waiting, giving her a chance to join in the conversation. She and him had been partners on that castle trip when they were eleven. After he'd dropped his glasses and someone else stepped on them, she'd led him up and down several flights of uneven stone spiral stairs with his hand on her shoulder, counting the steps out loud. His vision wasn't as bad as all that really, but it had been fun.

A small smile tugged at her lips, but before she could say anything, the door opened again and more sixth formers came in, loudly moaning about the rain. One of them switched on the little radio in the corner. The sound of the *Sugababes* filtered past Ziggy's earphones. Two noisy girls in lower-sixth came in and dropped their things onto the table next to her, chattering among themselves and ignoring her completely.

She turned her music up louder and leaned in closer to her sketchbook. Across the room, Luke and Jamie were joined by a few other friends. They were the loudest group by far. One of the other boys mussed up Jamie's wet hair, before producing a football from his backpack. Within minutes they were kicking it idly around between them.

Ziggy tensed. Footballs outside were bad enough, but footballs inside were even worse.

She didn't notice the boy approaching her across the sixth form lounge like a stray cat looking for scraps until he was right at her shoulder. He plucked an earphone from her ear.

"Hi."

Callum Blake. Professional pest.

The look she gave him should have communicated how rude she thought he was, but he seemed unperturbed and crouched next to her with a grin.

"What?" she asked scathingly.

"Not bad, that." He indicated her picture.

"Yeah, I know. What do you want?"

"Can you do me a favour?"

"I dunno."

She looked away from him, back to her picture, and he lowered his voice to a conspiratorial whisper, nudging her shoulder with his. He looked disheveled as usual, with brown hair in need of a trim, a creased shirt and strings of bracelets on his bony wrist. But he smelled like peppermints; a cover for cigarettes, Ziggy knew.

"Just hide something for me. Stokes is really on my case. I think they might search my locker this afternoon."

She twisted her mouth thoughtfully and looked at him sidelong. She didn't need to ask what it was.

"Why should I?"

"'Cause we're mates," he grinned. "'Cause you like me."

Half-truths were Callum's specialty. Ziggy scoffed, and he stuck out his bottom lip at her, making big eyes, and she couldn't help but laugh.

"Go on," he said earnestly. "Please, Ziggy."

He had copied her English homework once in year ten, changed it just enough to actually improve on it and get a better mark than her. He was new at the school then, plonked next to her at the start of term by virtue of the alphabet, having moved for reasons that changed every time in the telling. He didn't yet know that she was the class weirdo. As it turned out, he didn't seem to care. He was pretty weird himself.

Ziggy hesitated, glancing around the room full of noisy people. She wasn't sure if it was curiosity or bad habit that made her keep sitting next to him in Art lessons, but at least he kept his voice down when he spoke to her.

"Alright, fine. Just until the end of the day, though. There's space in my pencil box."

Under the table, she pulled her backpack closer so he could reach it and then leaned back across her sketchbook. She looked away while Callum reached into her bag to open her metal pencil tin and surreptitiously slip something inside.

Looking up from her sketch, she made eye contact with Jamie across the room, certain that he had noticed the exchange over Luke's shoulder. Her gut clenched, the kind of twist that came with being caught. Not in trouble, just… seen. She looked away quickly.

"Might have to be until tomorrow," said Callum quietly.

"What?" she shot him a dark look.

"Dunno if I'm going home tonight."

At least he had the grace to look contrite. Ziggy decided not to hold it against him. Not this time. She scowled at him, though.

"Fine."

His grin returned instantly. Though his pale eyes were too widely spaced to be considered good-looking, he had a nice smile.

"You're the best. I owe you one," he said.

"You owe me about five."

"I'm good for it. Name your price." He raised a brow, and she scoffed.

"You can start by going away. I'm busy."

"Aww, spoilsport. Alright, see you later."

She waited until he was gone to risk another look over at her old best friend.

Jamie had his back to her now, leaning against the chair that Luke was sat on. Reaching into the front pocket of her bag, she pulled out her phone and looked at her messages. She opened the one from Jamie. It was the first message he had sent her in some time, and even prior to that the conversation had always been somewhat one-sided.

Happy Bday Ziggy

She started typing out a response, then hesitated... What could she even say? *Thanks and sorry for ignoring you? Sorry I'm not the girl who led you up and down the stairs anymore?*

She deleted the message and put her phone away.

Chapter 4

It was raining in the churchyard, and the heavy clouds that obscured the moon made the sky blacker than spilled ink. Something growled, low and guttural from behind a headstone. Ziggy knew she was dreaming, but she didn't know how to wake herself up. With her back to the tall wooden door, the church loomed behind her like a grey gargoyle. She shivered.

It was hunting her, and she would have to face it.

She was dressed absurdly in a black dress with sparkly green stars that reached just below her knees, and a long black plastic cape dripping with raindrops. An old Halloween costume from when she was little. Her panicked breathing caught in her chest as she scanned the headstones. A dark shape slunk between them, crouched close to the ground, taut and ready to spring.

Then her eye caught another figure, ghostly and pale, escaping through the trees. A metallic tang of blood cut through the wet air. Claws scraped across the grass. With a burst of motion, the beast was off, chasing the pale shape into the trees. For a heartbeat, relief fluttered in her chest. It wasn't coming for her anymore.

But something was wrong.

She looked down.

Her fingers; plastic, green, with long black witch nails, were slick with blood that was still dripping.

* * *

Ziggy awoke with her heart hammering. Her eyes were swollen, face sticky with tears. Or was it sweat? Puck lay suffocatingly heavy on her chest, purring.

The cold grey morning light filtered in between her curtains, spilling across her cluttered bedside table.

Her phone bleeped.

Shifting to sit upright, much to Puck's annoyance, she reached out and pick it up. She had two text messages, both from Callum.

8:54am: **where r u**

11:12am: **looked 4 u this morning meet at ur locker b4 lunch**

Numbly, she typed a reply.

Not coming in. My Nana died last night.

Seeing the words made it real. A lump stuck in the back of her throat. Tears burned fresh. Callum's response was almost immediate.

shit sorry smoke it if u want

He should have been in class, but she imagined him hiding out behind the sports building, sitting on the high wall above the main road, alone, just watching cars go by.

Nah that's ok. Thanks tho

She sent the message, then rubbed at her eyes. The room was too quiet. Her stomach ached like there was a hole there so deep she might turn inside out. She curled up again, swallowed by the silence, and went back to sleep.

Chapter 5

Ziggy hadn't noticed before how faded the floral wallpaper was in Nana Peg's living room. She sat cross-legged on the floor, a cup of tea on the low table in front of her, steam rising from it in curling wisps. It was early morning, before nine o'clock, and still bleak with drizzling grey clouds outside. She'd walked over to her grandmother's house by herself, wanting to arrive before the rest of the family, to spend some time there alone before they stripped the place bare.

The crossword in last week's paper lay unfinished on the table, her own scrawl filling in half-hearted guesses. Peg used to love them until her eyesight went. These past few months, Ziggy would read out the clues, the letters jumbling on her tongue, and they'd muddle through them together.

It always took ages, but Nana Peg never minded, and neither did Ziggy.

Now, the name of the poet they'd struggled to remember came back to her, clear as day. She picked up the pen and inked in eight across: *John Keats*.

Next to the newspaper on the table was a folded card with a black-and-white photo of Peg as a young woman on the front. She wore her Land Army uniform proudly, and her smile had a touch of mischief, as though she was sharing a private joke with the person behind the camera. The caption read: In Loving Memory of Margaret Madeline Briggs, July 8th 1924- April 30th 2003.

Peter had read an extract from *The Little Prince* at the service, something nice about laughing at the stars, which Ziggy didn't think was quite right. Peg had never been sentimental. But her father insisted that it had been a favourite book of hers when she was a young woman.

Ziggy sat like a stone in the pew at the crematorium, in the green dress her grandmother had liked, wearing the locket with her own likeness inside. People she didn't know had patted her arm and said they couldn't believe she was all grown up, as though she didn't feel seven years old inside. There were no cheese and pickle sandwiches at the wake. She didn't eat anything, but neither did her mother, so at least it went unremarked on.

Finishing her tea, she took the cup out to the kitchen and washed it in the sink. There was another used cup and saucer already there, and a small side plate dusted with crumbs, so she washed those as well. She tried not to think about how it had been Peg's last cup of tea and slice of cake. Instead, she looked out at the garden, where rain misted the pale morning light.

The lavender wasn't blooming yet but come summer it would spill thick and fragrant across the garden wall. The green stalks were in bud, swaying in the damp morning breeze. The rhododendron was already ostentatiously pink, though, despite the drab weather, a bright pop of vibrancy in the bleak scene. The thick bush was heavy with blossoms. Ziggy tilted her head, a strange prickling creeping up her spine.

In the shadowed tangle of branches, a pair of yellow eyes stared back.

Her breath caught.

She blinked hard, and they were gone. Just rain-speckled glass and shivering leaves.

A cat, maybe. Or a trick of the light. That was all.

She shook off the image. Her nerves were raw, and she hadn't slept well. Even though they had known it was coming, Peg's death still felt sudden. Peaceful, quiet, in her sleep, but sudden.

She kept cleaning. Time blurred in a fog of soap suds and memories until the front door cracked open at around nine-thirty, and her brother and father appeared.

Peter put a pile of empty cardboard boxes on the table and flicked the kettle on, smiling cautiously at Ziggy. His mop of dark curls was damp with rain.

"You okay?"

"Uh-huh."

"What time did you get here?" asked their father, hanging his wet jacket on the back of a wooden dining chair.

"Early."

Gary and Peter exchanged a look. Ziggy folded her arms. "Where shall we start?" she asked.

"With a cuppa," replied Gary airily. "There's biscuits want eating, eh?"

"Is Mum coming?"

"Not this morning, sweetheart. Not feeling up to it. You can sort through Nana's books, can't you?"

"I... yeah," she replied uncertainly. "But Mum would know better what's worth selling, wouldn't she? I think Nana had some first editions..."

"You'll figure it out," said Gary, in a placating tone. Ziggy frowned.

Didn't he care?

In a previous life, June Briggs had worked for a large publishing house, and over the years, she'd used her connections to gift Peg rare first editions on birthdays and Christmases. But kidney disease had forced her to give up work when Ziggy was too young to *really* understand. The quiet, bookish version of her mother, who rarely left the house now, was easier to talk to than the driven, fast-paced woman she barely remembered. But sometimes just *looking* at her could make Ziggy feel exhausted.

The caravan had solved the problem of June's struggles with housekeeping and the mess caused by her daughter's art.

Ziggy didn't care to admit- even to herself- how often she hid there to avoid her mother, but this task felt too big. *What if she missed something important? What if she gave away something rare without realising?*

"Come on, don't look like that," said Gary gently. He had biscuit crumbs in his beard again. "Let's get this done, eh? To be honest, I reckon your Nana already got rid of everything that wanted getting rid of. She knew it was coming, didn't she?"

It disturbed her how businesslike he was being, even with his soft words and kind smile.

She nodded, picked up the boxes, and walked into the living room; into the heart of Peg's world, ready to pull it apart piece by piece.

Chapter 6

Ziggy's stomach grumbled. She hadn't even realised she was hungry, so fixated was she on the tiny spots of *Titan Buff* mixed with a minuscule amount of *Violet Oxide* that she was adding to leaf shapes on the canvas to suggest raindrops. Now, suddenly, her body cried out for food.

The caravan door opened, and as though summoned by her growling stomach, Peter came in with a covered plate and a steaming mug of milky tea.

"Mum said you'd be wanting this about now," he said, handing her the plate. He set the mug down on the table among her paints as she lifted the cover to see a crispy, golden toasted sandwich.

"Ta."

Situating herself on the squashy foam seat at the table, she folded her legs up and began tucking into the sandwich with gusto. Peter looked around the caravan with wide eyes, taking in the papers stuck to the walls with Blu-Tack. He lingered on a pencil sketch of a hand, wrinkled, with arthritis-swollen knuckles.

"Did she ever come see this? Your little studio?" he asked. Ziggy shook her head, her mouth too full of gooey cheese. "It's brilliant. She loved your work, y'know."

She nodded. "What is this you're working on?" he gestured to the canvas. "For your coursework? Is there a story behind it?"

She wiped tangy pickle from the corner of her mouth.

"I'm not sure," she said. "Sometimes I have dreams, and then I paint them. I don't even know what that's meant to be..." she pointed to the slight, shadowy figure at the side of the canvas. The shape of the limbs suggested movement, and it looked back over its shoulder at the wolf pursuing it. The outline of the body was clear, but it still wore a ghastly pale face, with black smudges for eyes.

"When I planned the painting, I had a whole sketch outlined for a stag I was going to put there, but then last week for some reason, I just decided to change it and now I'm not sure what I'm doing. I think I might have ruined it..." she frowned thoughtfully. "What do you think it looks like?"

"You're asking me?" Peter scoffed. He moved to get a closer look, then stood back again, brow furrowed thoughtfully. "A ghost maybe...I don't know, it needs more detail."

Ziggy gave a little huff of annoyance and stood up again.

"I know *that*," she said.

Her brother reached out to pick up a sketch book from the pile on the table, then hesitated.

"Can I look at some of these?" he asked.

Raising an eyebrow, Ziggy turned back to her painting. Peter had never shown any interest in her art before. She supposed he was feeling maudlin. Or guilty.

"Fine, but I don't appreciate unsolicited opinions," she told him sourly.

"Unsolicited?" He laughed, taking a seat at the table with the book. "You just asked me what I thought."

Ziggy said nothing. She stared at the canvas, hand hovering in mid-air, searching for the next raindrop, but her brother's page-turning distracted her. She heard him chuckle and looked over her shoulder to see the page he was looking at. A sketch of Puck, her dappled coat rendered in black ink, yawning and stretching her paws out in front of her, a pair of soft feathery wings jutting from her shoulders in a wide arc.

"I love that," said Peter, smiling. The next pages had a few less successful portraits of the cat, studies of her eyes and teeth. Ziggy had been toying with lots of different ideas for animals to include in her painting before settling on the beast and the stag and this book was full of experimental sketches. He stopped on a page filled with many different types of eyes staring out from it. Human eyes, cat eyes, stag eyes, wolf eyes, monstrous eyes, all vividly scratched in black ink on the white paper, as though the book itself were alive with consciousness. Peter scrunched up his nose.

"Y'know... if you decide on York, you don't have to stay in halls... I've got a spare room..."

She looked around at him in surprise, but he had turned his head back to the pictures stuck on the wall, examining them closely.

"Did Robbie move out?" she asked.

Peter didn't answer. For a long moment he was very still, the muscles in his neck tense and his hand paused, uncurling the corner of a sketch of the old apple tree that stood at the edge of the village near the train tracks.

"No," he said eventually.

The tightness of his voice alarmed her slightly.

"Oh..."

He turned around, and she saw that his blue eyes, so like her own, mirrored her anxiety.

"Mum and Dad don't know…" he said and cleared his throat. "I mean… I wanted to suggest it to you first… you might tell me to mind my own business, I dunno…" he ran a hand through his dark hair, offered her a weak smile. "I just feel like we could both use a friend. And I think you and Robbie would get on. He's pretty into *Lord of the Rings* and stuff…"

Ziggy laughed a little at that. She could see the panic starting to ebb on her brother's face and she gave a tiny nod.

"Thanks… I'll think about it."

"You're welcome," said Peter. He picked up the sketchbook again and idly flipped over the page. "Speaking of *Lord of the Rings*. Who's this?"

"It's not from *Lord of the*…"

At the sight of the sketch, Ziggy dropped her paintbrush. Peter had put the book down dismissively and was collecting dirty cups from the counter.

"Mum's been looking for this mug, y'know," he said pulling a face as he poured cold dregs of tea into the sink. "You're a right minger, you."

Ziggy's eyes were on the sketchbook and the shadowy face that stared out from it. Shrouded in a hood of moss, the wild-haired creature had fiery eyes and a pair of white antlers protruding like twisted spears from his head. She recognised her own hand in the lines, but the thing that stopped her cold was that she had no memory of drawing it.

It was her ink, her sketchbook, her familiar lines; but the shape of the face made her chest tight. She knew those antlers. She'd drawn them before, maybe. But not like this. Not with that expression. Not with those eyes.

"What's up?" Peter asked her.

Ziggy shook her head, feeling foolish. Of course she had drawn it. And hundreds just like it. She usually remembered them all, but after all these years was it really so surprising to forget just one? Maybe she had wanted to forget this one because of the sickly creeping feeling it caused in her stomach.

"Nothing," she said, closing the book. But her hand trembled on the cover.

Chapter 7

Surrounded by cardboard boxes, stacks of books, china ornaments and bubble wrap, Ziggy sat in Nana Peg's living room, boxing up her childhood and sealing it away with brown parcel tape. She yawned and stretched her back. She had stayed up far too late the night before, poring over her sketchbook in her bedroom, trying to recreate the blazing eyes of the antlered man from her drawing. She drew his face again and again, but it never looked as fierce, or as alive, as the sketch she couldn't even remember making.

Her fingers were sore and stained this morning and her book lay on the table along with another pile of old ones unearthed from under Peg's bed. Some were full of recent, skilful renderings of creatures with delicate wings and sharp teeth, moss for hair and leaves growing from their skin. Others were older. Scratchy pencil drawings from her childhood; fairies carrying giant teeth, pointy-eared elves sitting under trees laden with blood red apples.

She carefully slid a bubble-wrapped glass vase into a box. As a child, she would have loved this. Peg would have made it fun. In fact, she remembered helping her grandmother pack up her old house, a three-bedroom semi near the school in the heart of the village, when the stairs and the upkeep got too much for her. Wrapping each trinket in newspaper, she'd told Little Justine a fanciful story about it.

"I keep her high on the mantle so that her little ones can't escape," she said of a delicate white china shepherdess with three sweet lambs at her skirts. "She came from your Grandpa Gwyn's house. Remember the mining village I told you about? She's used to letting them roam the hills, isn't she? I've tried telling her she's not in the valleys anymore, but I don't speak Welsh. So, I keep her up high on that shelf, that way nobody can wander off." Peg had twinkled a smile, and Justine's eyes went wide with wonder. She always kept an eye on that shepherdess and her lambs after that, even as she grew up and came to understand that Nana Peg was full of these types of stories.

Smiling faintly at the memory, Ziggy picked up the shepherdess to wipe the dust from her with a cloth, making sure all the crevices around her arms and bonnet were clean, as well as the tiny lambs faces. She was disappointed to find the shepherdess' wooden base wobbly.

"What's wrong?" asked Gary, walking through from the bedroom with a black plastic sack full of clothes and seeing the look on her face. She held up the shepherdess and gave the base a wobble to show him. "It's meant to do that," he said. "Twist it."

Perplexed, Ziggy carefully began to twist the base and found that it turned easily, clicking, winding up some mechanism inside. The shepherdess was musical. She placed it down on the coffee table and it slowly began to rotate, playing a lilting tune. Each note rang clear; no sign of damage after all these years. But the melody was slow, laced with minor notes that gave it a mournful sweetness.

"It's a Welsh folk song, Dad used to know the words, all I

remember is the 'fal di ral' part. Translates to something like 'my sweetheart is in the orchard'. It was very lovely."

When he said the word 'lovely', there was a trace of an accent in his voice and Ziggy smiled.

"I think I remember it now," she said. "Nana used to play it for me when I was little, but I always wanted to mess about with it. That's probably why she put it up on the high shelf, so I wouldn't break it."

"Probably," agreed Gary.

"Can I keep it?"

"Course you can, love."

There was a sound of voices from the next room and the front door closing. Ziggy followed her father into the kitchen where Peter stood with packing paper in hand. Jamie Cleary was with him, in shorts despite the weather, a red leisure centre tee visible beneath his raincoat. It was Saturday morning and there would probably be a plethora of swimming lessons and children's birthday parties waiting for him at work today.

"Alright, Baywatch?" said Ziggy, and he smiled.

"Hiya, Ziggy… how are you?"

"I'm okay," she shrugged, looking at his feet. He had much cleaner Reeboks these days than he used to.

"I just wanted to come over and see you. I was really sorry to hear about Nana Peg, I…" he hesitated, fidgeted with the cuff of his coat. "She was always good to me, when I was growing up. We used to come and see her all the time, didn't we…"

The silence widened between them and Jamie looked away.

"Thanks Jamie," said Gary. "She was really fond of you actually," he chuckled. "She always said you did a better job on the grass than your brother."

Jamie's smile returned easily.

"That reminds me, I found something," said Ziggy. She nodded toward the living room, beckoning him to follow. "Watch out for the pokers."

Jamie swerved to avoid a cast iron fireplace set that had been left in the middle of the room. Ziggy went to the sideboard and picked up the red packet she had placed there earlier after finding it inside the cupboard. An open pack of four Kit Kat Chunky, with one missing, and a yellow Post-it note attached that read, in Peg's swirly handwriting. *Jamie Cleary grass cutting.*

"I think these are for you," said Ziggy, handing it to him.

Jamie let out a soft laugh.

"She used to pay me two pound every time," he said. "When I got a bit older, I told her not to bother... Then one time she gave me one of these, and I said they were my favourite. After that she always had one for me, every time I cut the grass... I didn't know she bought them special."

Ziggy felt a lump in her throat and was suddenly overcome with panic at the thought of crying in front of him. It was all too surreal. Standing in this room she knew so well, with him, the only person she had never been afraid to speak her mind to when they were children, surrounded by all these pieces of a life, packed away into boxes like so many small coffins.

And here they were. Grown-ups, technically. Practically strangers.

"I'm sorry I never texted you back the other week," she murmured. *I'm sorry for all the times I never texted you back.*

"Don't worry about it," he said quickly. "Is this what you're working on?" He gestured to the pile of sketchbooks on the table. There was one open on top with the cover folded back, the first page was a pencil sketch, a gnarled tree with long, grey limbs, heavy with apples. The tree at the edge of the village, near the train tracks. It wasn't as well done as the one stuck to the wall in the caravan, she could see where her skills had refined, but it was easily recognisable as that tree, if you knew it as well as they both did.

"No, those are old," she said. "I haven't drawn that tree in years."

"We stopped going there, didn't we, after... that time you got hurt."

Silence followed, and all the words she wanted to say burned Ziggy's throat. Her father and brother hadn't followed them into the living room, but even though they were alone, it still seemed impossible to acknowledge the truth of what they had seen and endured four years ago, out past that apple tree.

"Here's some newer stuff." She picked up the book she'd been drawing in the night before, the one with all her practice sketches and studies for the animals in the wood and flipped it open to a page with the stag. "I've been working on this for my portfolio piece, but I don't think I'm going to use it."

"Oh, wow, that's really cool..." Smiling, Jamie took the sketchbook. He turned the page to the next sketch, a study of the stag's face and antlers. "Why aren't you going to use it?"

"Uh, I'm not sure really..." she shrugged. "My inspiration just... went a different direction, I s'pose."

He turned the page again and something in his expression changed. It was an ink drawing of the beast, emerging from darkness, sharp white teeth bared towards the viewer, its hackles raised in awareness of being observed. Jamie didn't say anything, but he had gone very still.

"That's what I've been painting," said Ziggy carefully. "I couldn't decide what it was meant to be hunting. At first it was the stag, but now I'm not sure... Are you okay?"

"What? Yeah." Jamie blinked and closed the book. "It's really cool, Ziggy. Just... dark."

But she saw the look in his eyes. Not just surprise. *Recognition. Fear.*

Disorientated, Ziggy forced a laugh. She needed to change the subject.

"I know. Weird, right? But, hey, I drew you too. Hang on, I'll find it." She went back to the pile of books on the coffee table, flicked through a couple before finding what she was looking for. "I don't even remember when I did this, maybe year nine... here..."

She opened the book to a page with another ink drawing. A shadow of a tree loomed over a figure, a scrawny boy with dark hair dressed all in black. The only splash of colour was the orange pumpkin-shaped bucket in his hand. His face was ghostly white, made up like a skeleton, but messily done, as though the child had rubbed at it. The eyes, big black circles around them, were bright with unspilled tears and the mouth turned down gloomily. It was Jamie, in his Halloween costume from when they were seven years old.

He looked at it like it was a portrait of a dead man. Ziggy had meant to lighten the mood but now she regretted showing it to him.

"Wow," he said. "I don't know whether to feel honoured or depressed..."

She realised he was teasing her, and she laughed.

"I'll tell my biographers not to bother interviewing you then, shall I?"

"Nah, I've got all the best stories."

"Yeah, you do." *Now Nana Peg is gone.*

Jamie smiled at her, and for a moment, they were children again.

"I've got to go to work, my bus is in five minutes," he said. "You're not getting rid of all these sketch books, are you?"

"I'm not sure. There's so many."

"Think of your biographers though."

Ziggy shrugged, laughing.

"Can I at least have this one?" He held up the book with the skeleton drawing.

"Yeah, alright."

"There's nothing embarrassing in it, is there?" he grinned. "No more drawings of me? No emo diary entries about how much you wanted to kiss me in year nine?"

"Piss off, Funnybones." She laughed.

"Alright, I'm going. It's good to talk to you, Ziggy. Can we hang out soon?"

"Sure."

He waved from the door with the book and was gone. Ziggy turned back to the coffee table and picked up her newest sketch book. She sat down on the sofa and turned to the page that had caused Jamie to react so strangely. She knew that the wolf was a grim image, but he'd looked at it like it wasn't just a drawing. Like it was real. Like it had followed him here.

Her stomach squirmed with unease. There was something she was missing. Ziggy blinked at the door he had just gone out of.

And then she realised it.

The skeleton.

The pale, ghoulish monster in her painting; drawn from somewhere deep in her dreaming mind. Now she knew exactly what that figure was supposed to be. It wasn't a ghost at all. It was a memory. A boy in a costume, pale and forlorn.

It was Jamie.

Chapter 8

R U home

Why?

meet me by the church

what? when?

now

Im busy

no ur not

The sky was starting to turn bluish grey as the sun disappeared behind the rows of smart Victorian semis opposite the church.

"What are you doing here?" Ziggy asked. Callum's smile was mellow as he stood up on the pedals of his bike, rolling towards her before dismounting.

"Had nowhere better to go," he replied lightly.

Callum lived on an estate at the edge of the town centre, a good half-hour bike ride from the village and his bike was the grubbiest piece of scrap metal Ziggy had ever seen. The back tyre was balding, its spokes speckled with rust. He didn't look much better, if she was honest. There was a fresh rip in the knee of his jeans, definitely not the kind her mother would scornfully call 'fashionably distressed.' He was wearing a red tee shirt with the logo for the album *White Pony* on the front, but no jacket, though. There were inky doodles on the skin of his forearm, faded but not completely washed off. A new bracelet of colourful plastic beads stood out among the fraying leather and braided silk that usually wrapped his wrist.

He leaned his bike against the wall of the churchyard.

"Missed you last week. You okay?"

"No, you didn't, you just want this."

Ziggy, bundled up in a hoodie against the evening chill, pulled it up over her long plaits. She produced the little plastic sandwich bag from her pocket and handed it to him, grateful to be rid of it. He grinned at her and immediately went into his own pocket to fish out a packet of Golden Virginia and liquorice Rizla.

"You're gonna do that here?" she asked, looking around. Callum peered up and down the empty street. It was getting dark and only a fat pigeon gazed down from the tree above, cooing softly. He shrugged.

"Can go in there if you like." He gestured with a thumb over the wall into the churchyard and Ziggy rolled her eyes. "Come on," he said with a grin. "Let's have a look. I could use some more inspiration for my final piece."

Callum's level of enthusiasm for art lessons wavered along with his attendance. There was no doubting his talent. Like Ziggy, he was particularly good at pencil and ink drawings, and like her, his tastes ran to the macabre and weird.

He had an aptitude for drawing architecture, and often submitted pictures of churches, gothic buildings with sharp spires and grotesque gargoyles, but regularly his work was unfinished, late or simply forgotten. He rarely contributed in lessons, usually appeared to not even be paying attention, drawing swirling patterns on his own hands and arms. Then occasionally he would surprise everyone by turning in an incredibly skilled and thoughtful piece of work that nobody knew he was capable of.

"Can we climb over?" he asked, looking up at the wall.

"The gate's just down there," she pointed.

Callum wheeled his bike down the path to the corner of the street, pausing under the glow of the streetlamp to look around again.

"So, are you alright?" he asked as she followed him through the high wrought-iron gate. Earlier that day, the bells had tolled their regular call, and a dozen or so faithful patrons had attended Sunday mass at the church, but in the dim evening light, the churchyard felt abandoned and bleak.

"I'm cold," she said, folding her arms. "Aren't you?"

"Not really," he said, and she knew she wasn't fooling him by dodging the question, but he let it go. "Do you ever come in here? Which one's your house?"

"My garden's over that wall," she pointed towards the mossy wall, near the back corner of the churchyard, where it curved around the small stone building. Beyond the wall, on the other side of the building, there was woodland, and these were the ancient yew trees that loomed heavily over the garden and Ziggy's caravan. "I came in here once, years ago with Lena, in the middle of the night. We were trying to scare each other."

There was a faint smell of damp earth and decaying leaves. The whisper of wind through the trees made her shiver. Callum left his bike leaning against a tall headstone and hopped up onto the wall that lined the path to the door of the church to sit and roll his joint, sprinkling the crumby green stuff out of the little packet in with the rolling tobacco with a practiced hand. The grass was well kept, but the headstones were rough and weathered, a few with ivy crawling all over long forgotten names.

"I've been dreaming about it lately, though," Ziggy admitted, uncomfortably. She climbed up onto the wall next to him. Despite the dampness soaking through her jeans, she preferred to keep the high wall at her back and Callum at her side. Although she wasn't sure encouraging closeness with him was a good idea, or how he might interpret it. He didn't appear to even notice, as he lit the joint and took a slow drag.

"About what? The churchyard?"

"Yeah... I think it's because of this painting I'm working on. It's kind of creepy."

That got Callum's attention. He blew smoke with an amused look on his face.

"Oh yeah? What's creepy enough to give *you* nightmares?"

"It's not just that. It's probably because of my Nana as well... it's got me thinking about dark stuff.... Stuff that happened years ago that's hard to forget, y'know?"

Callum's face had fallen. He took another drag and looked down at his hands. He fiddled with the beads on his wrist, pastel pink and blue. Some of them were heart-shaped and others had letters stamped on them but didn't spell out anything that made sense: CHOXXX.

"You mean when Lena's brother died?" he asked quietly. "I heard about that. It was the year before I moved here, wasn't it?"

She nodded.

The earthy, fruity smell of his smoke had made the muscles in her back and neck soften and she leaned against him a little, but in her mind's eye she saw the gore-soaked Converse trainer floating in the stream. The sunflower yellow hair dripping blood. An involuntary shudder rippled down her back.

"What was your dream about?"

Callum's pupils were huge. He held out the joint to her, but she shook her head.

"Nothing," she said. "It's stupid."

He gave her a calculating look, then smiled lazily.

"I'll tell you my dream," he offered, like it was a bargaining chip. He stubbed out the joint against the wall although there was still half left and wrapped it up in the Golden Virginia packet before tucking it away in his pocket. Ziggy scoffed.

"No thanks," she said. "I don't want to know what goes on in your head."

Except she sort of did.

Callum laughed and slid down from the wall.

"Are you gonna show me your creepy painting, then?" he asked.

"Alright, but I don't take criticism."

She jumped down after him, disarmed again by his casual acceptance of her rebuff and mostly pleased to be leaving the churchyard. It was starting to mist with rain again. She licked her lips, tasting a sharp metallic tang in the chilly evening air as she scuffed along after him. He picked up his bike, the tyres scraping on the ground and just then a sound cut through the shadows. A low vibrating growl.

It didn't sound like a dog. Or if it did, it was a dog made of gravel and grave-dirt. It rumbled, distorted; like it had come from beneath the ground.

Ziggy's stomach twisted. Her hand shot out, catching Callum's arm before her brain caught up and he spun around, pale eyes wide.

"-the fuck..."

He dropped the bike in alarm, and it clattered on the crunchy stones. The growl rose to a bark, sharp and vicious. Ziggy's eyes darted about in a panic, seeking the source. "Let's go," Callum hissed. "Now."

He picked up his bike again but shoved her ahead of him along the path to the gate.

Ziggy sprinted. The bark chased them. Angry. Wild. Callum was at her heels, the wheels of his bike dragging frantically.

Clang.

The church bell tolled. A yelp escaped Ziggy's throat. She stumbled. Out the gate, around the corner, up the path. Twenty metres. That was all.

Breathless, more from the fright than the short run, she halted at the gate of the red brick house. The curtains glowed in the bay window, friendly and safe. The bells continued to chime. Ten o'clock. There was no sign of anything behind them. She turned to Callum.

"What was that? Did you see it?"

He shook his head, breathing hard.

"I didn't see anything. I heard…" he kept shaking his head. "I dunno. I'm a bit stoned." He coughed a little, and it turned into a laugh. "One of your neighbours has got a seriously mean fucking dog. That really shit me up… Are you okay?"

Ziggy realised she was still gripping his arm tightly and, feeling foolish, she let go. Somehow, he'd managed to push his bike with one arm while she dragged him by the other. Callum started to laugh properly, and the sound washed the adrenaline right through her body. She laughed too, giddy from the rush.

"We're such idiots," she said. Callum grinned and although his pupils were still big, his shoulders relaxed. "Leave your bike down the side, and be quiet," she warned.

She led him around the side of the house, into the overgrown back garden, dripping with as much ivy as rainwater. The caravan door creaked open, and she flicked on the lights. It was wired with electricity via a hook up which was powered by the house's main supply. Her parents had long given up questioning her about coming down here at night. Callum looked around in awe.

"This is proper good," he beamed. "I would literally never go home if I had one of these."

"Sometimes I don't," she admitted.

Then his eyes found the wolf painting, perched on its easel like a predator waiting for them, and his smile vanished.

"You're right, that is creepy," he said. "Is that what you've been dreaming about?"

Ziggy nodded without looking at him. She sat down at the table and fiddled with a palette, scratching at a speck of dried paint with a fingernail. "No wonder you got freaked out when you heard that dog," Callum conceded with a nod. "This is really good though, y'know?"

"Thanks… but… can I ask you something weird?"

"Sure." He was still examining the painting, looking closely at the pale skeletal figure.

"Have you ever drawn something that… that you didn't know where it came from? Like… that you didn't even know was in your head?"

"Like automatic drawing? Sure," he shrugged. "That's the only way I know how to do it."

Unsure if he was joking, she decided not to pursue that thought.

"I just… feel like lately I'm not the one in control of what I draw…" He was looking at her oddly, and she shook her head.

"Never mind, I'm not making any sense."

Callum frowned thoughtfully, his eyes roving around the various pictures stuck to the walls of the caravan.

"I know what you mean though, this coursework is hard, trying to figure out what it's supposed to *mean*..." he made air-quotes with his fingers. "GCSE was like 'look at this tree I drew'... A-level is like 'here's a painting of a rotting windowsill, it represents my unresolved trauma'..."

Ziggy's lips twitched. He looked serious though. "If there's something you're missing... Maybe it's just... your brain showing you what you already know..." Ziggy raised her eyebrows, unconvinced, but the look Callum gave her was astute. "Like, maybe it's your life that's out of control."

She felt his words like a rock in her stomach. He might have a point.

But he was also stoned.

She pulled a face at him.

"Fuck off Callum, I don't like you."

She expected him to laugh, but his eye had been caught by one of her pictures. The apple tree.

"I know this place," he said slowly, a crease appearing between his eyebrows. "Out by the train tracks, yeah? First summer after I moved here, I came up to the village on my bike one day... There were so many apples on that tree." He touched the twisted branches with a finger as inky as Ziggy's. "I ate one and I swear it must have had pesticide on it or something. I felt so weird... I passed out in the grass, like fast asleep."

A small smile crept across his features at the memory, as though he still couldn't believe it. He moved to sit down on the seat opposite her across the table. "It was dark by the time I woke up. I don't even know how long I was asleep... I got home so late my mum had locked the door."

Ziggy stood up, suddenly anxious, and moved across the caravan to pour herself a drink of water, but really it was to put some space between herself and Callum.

She looked at him. *Really* looked at him. There was a glaze over his eyes, dull and hazy, like he wasn't quite *there* anymore. Her skin prickled. She didn't know if it was fear or pity that she felt for him, but it made her squirm uncomfortably. Her hand went to the locket at her neck, seeking something familiar.

Callum tilted his head back against the window listlessly, looking up at the ceiling, and ran both hands through his messy hair. The skin on his right elbow was raw with a fresh graze that looked like a carpet burn.

He'd come over on his bike, three miles and most of it busy roads with no cycle path at dusk. For the first time, she really wondered why.

"You okay?" she asked.

He looked up with mild surprise, eyes slightly unfocused. "I asked you first."

"No," she admitted, feeling oddly exposed under his unsteady gaze. "I'm not."

"Me neither," he replied, but then like the flick of a switch, his smile was back. "Can I crash here? I promise I'll be gone before anyone's up."

"Callum..."

"Please? I'll owe you six."

He was smiling as though he was making a joke, perfectly at ease and knew just how charming he was, but there was a faint hint of something else in his eyes.

I had nowhere better to go.

"Okay," she said. "But you seriously better be gone, my Dad

gets up early and I mean *early*."

"That's fine, I dunno if I'll sleep with *Scooby Doo* staring at me anyway," he gestured to the painting and Ziggy laughed lightly.

She stood up to leave but Callum turned and caught her arm before she got to the door. For a moment she wondered if he was about to try to kiss her, but he blinked lethargically, and she saw just how drawn his face was.

"Thanks, Ziggy," he said. "You're a good friend."

"Yeah, I am. Would you tell Miss Tucker that? Get her off my back about being more sociable, since you owe me six?"

Callum laughed mid-yawn, scrubbing a hand over his face. "Sure."

Ziggy closed the door of the caravan, feeling exhausted, and despite knowing that there was nothing out there in the dark, she still thought she could smell wet fur.

Chapter 9

Ziggy could tell her mother had made an effort. It was only toast and scrambled eggs, but the golden slices glistened with butter, and the eggs crackled in the pan as she came down the stairs. Peter sipped coffee at the table while Gary put together his lunch for work.

It wasn't just the food; it was the fact that June was up and dressed. She looked tired, but not grey or sickly. And it wasn't just because Peter was leaving today, either. Ziggy was going back to school, and Gary was going back to work. A-level exams started in less than two weeks, and the world continued to turn.

The night before, eyes stinging with exhaustion, Ziggy had lain awake in bed, trying to tell herself she wasn't listening out for the howl of a wolf in the garden below. Shortly after midnight, unable to shake the unease in her stomach, she got up and went to the window to look out over the trees. She pressed her forehead to the cold glass. All was still below, the caravan dark and quiet beneath the misty rain. Callum had barely been able to keep his eyes open, and she imagined he'd been asleep before she even reached the back door. She just hoped he was an early riser. Sure enough, as the sky began to turn pink and she leaned out her bedroom window to look, his bike was gone.

Her mother was asking her a question. She blinked, fork halfway to her mouth.

"Sorry, what?"

"What time are you meeting your English teacher, do you remember?"

"First thing. I've got a free lesson. It was mostly revision stuff I missed last week anyway, but I want to catch up."

"And Art?"

"I'll talk to Miss Tucker later today. I'm not behind. I've been texting some people from my class, so…"

"Oh?" June's eyebrows went up, as though quietly alarmed at the revelation that her daughter actually had friends.

"Yeah, you remember Fliss?"

Mentioning Callum would be a mistake.

"Oh… yes." June poured another cup of tea and sat down opposite her. "So, you're going to be alright, sweetheart?"

Peter rolled his eyes.

"Mum, leave her alone, would you? She's going back to school, not the Gulf of Iraq."

Ziggy shot him a grateful smile as she finished her breakfast. His hug goodbye at the door when she left to catch the bus was brief but sincere. "Have a think about September, yeah?"

"Yeah, okay. Thanks…say hi to Robbie from me."

He smiled.

* * *

On her way to meet her English teacher, she took the long way behind the sports hall; not looking for Callum exactly, just checking if he might be there. A pair of year eleven boys were sat on the wall overlooking the road passing a cigarette between them, they glanced at her suspiciously, then turned back around. She kept walking. She took out her phone, considered texting him, but put it away again.

Felicity was waiting by her locker with a handful of printouts from art and a week's worth of gossip, both delivered at high speed with absolutely no context.

"I'm literally only telling you this because I know you don't care; but you know Wonderbra Rachel?"

"No?"

"Yes, you do. She's in my form, not yours. The one with the drawn-on eyebrows."

Ziggy nodded vaguely, only catching every third word.

"Anyway. She's going out with Mark something, I don't know him, but apparently, they were at McDonalds in town on Monday night…"

Across the corridor, she saw Jamie coming out of the sixth form lounge, slouching under the weight of a kit bag and nodding while Motormouth Luke jabbered at him, arms waving to articulate a point. He raised his hand in a silent greeting. She offered a weak smile in return. He looked pale and unwell, dragging his feet. He followed Luke off down the corridor with the resigned air of someone who should have stayed in bed that morning but had coursework to finish.

"Oh! And did you hear about Amelia Taylor's dog?"

"What?" Ziggy's head snapped around.

"It got killed. She lives in your village, doesn't she?"

"Yeah, just around the corner…"

Felicity pulled a face and spoke quietly.

"Yeah, so a few nights ago, they found it ripped to shreds at the bottom of the garden. Stupid little Pomeranian thing or something… but still."

"Jesus…"

Ziggy remembered the churchyard. The vicious growl. The smell of wet fur. Her stomach turned.

"Yeah… Might wanna keep an eye on your cat."

Chapter 10

The rhythm of the rock music in Ziggy's ears drowned out the sound of chatter in the sixth form lounge. Ignoring the other girls already sprawled on the sofa at the low table in the back corner, she dropped to the floor, tucking her legs under herself. One girl shifted her belongings to make space for her but didn't acknowledge Ziggy's presence.

She flipped open her sketchbook and blinked again at the wild-haired antlered man staring back at her. The skin on the back of her neck prickled. She turned the page, past the rough redrawing from the other night, and started a clean sheet.

She took a bite of her sandwich and started drawing, trying not to think too hard about it. *What had Callum called it? Automatic drawing; letting your hand draw without thinking.* Her hand moved across the page, the pencil making sharp lines.

A laugh cut through the air and Ziggy flinched. She turned her music up louder. Her blazer felt too hot. She straightened her spine, rolled her shoulders, and put pencil back to paper. Her hand moved faster now, urgent.

Her phone buzzed in her pocket. Probably Callum, asking her to cover for him in art again. She sighed and frowned at the screen. It was from Jamie.

Can I talk to you? After school

She hesitated for a long time before typing a response.

OK. C u @ the bus stop

They never used to have to ask. Jamie would always wait for her at the bus stop after school. Sometimes they'd go to the corner shop. She'd get a can of Sprite or a packet of Skittles and share them with him on the wall by his house. Sometimes they'd meet Lena and Nicky at the park. The boys were better at the monkey bars than she was, but when Nicky challenged her to see who could sit on the roundabout the longest and spin without getting dizzy, she always won.

Once, in year seven, in the bitter grip of winter, powered by sugar and resentment, the four of them had hidden in the bushes and pelted a pair of boys in the year above them with snowballs. The boys were the ringleaders of a group that found Ziggy's sketchbook hilarious every time they stole it from her. Nicky was always righteous about stuff like that, although he never even looked at Ziggy's drawings; not the way Jamie did. Jamie actually told her they were cool.

Lena was… different, before her brother died. Before that strange summer when everything turned upside-down and they all suddenly grew up. Lena had always been quiet and unassertive; her twin's pretty shadow. Then she vanished. Not like kids move away or grow apart. Lena… stopped being Lena. The way Nana Peg used to talk about changelings from under the hill. How they take your name and your voice and leave something twisted behind.

Ziggy shuddered at the memory.

The thing that came back wasn't Lena. Ziggy *knew* it. *Jamie* knew it. She'd drawn it over and over. Something with hawk eyes and sharp teeth wearing Lena's face.

When Lena- the real Lena- returned to them like a migrating

bird and saw the drawings, she cried. She said it wasn't true.

"You do remember," Ziggy had accused. She'd poked Jamie in the chest. "*You* were there."

Her phone buzzed again. Callum.

woof

She snorted; annoyance, or maybe relief. Around her, people were standing and slinging bags over their shoulders. She'd missed the bell. She pulled out her earphones and glanced at her sketchbook. The antlered man had returned, rough and dark among the trees. His hair blew in the wind. One arm stretched out, cloaked in moss and fur, pointing into the distance.

The beast ran ahead of him, eyes glowing, jaw slack with hunger.

***

Ziggy stood at the back of the crowd waiting to board the school bus, earphones in, music playing, when she heard someone say her name. She blinked with surprise to see Lena at her shoulder. She pulled out an earphone. Only one.

"Hi," Lena smiled. It wasn't awkward or forced. It was kind. Friendly. Ziggy hated that she had never learned to smile that way. "I wanted to say…" the smile left her mouth, but her eyes stayed soft. "I heard about your Nan. I'm sorry. She was so lovely. You must really-"

"Thanks, Lena."

Lena faltered, mouth open ready to continue, but Ziggy saw an opportunity to escape and shouldered past a few year eights.

"Luke! Got any chewing gum?"

"Why? Your breath stink?"

"Yep."

He grinned at her and offered a pack from his pocket. She took one but pulled a face.

"Airwaves? What is *wrong* with you?"

"Definitely not nasal congestion."

She climbed the steps onto the bus behind him, spotting Jamie take a seat near the middle. She thought about going up to sit across the aisle from him, since he said he wanted to talk to her, but watched him put up his hood and rest his head back against the seat wearily. *What did he even want to talk about?* She chose a seat near the front and let out a silent breath of relief when Lena carried on up the aisle past her.

Luke, on the other hand, dropped into the seat directly opposite, even though there were plenty of others free, as though this were the menthol section. She stared out of the window, watching trees and road signs blur past, trying to ignore him, but she could feel his eyes on her.

"Jamie looks rough, have you seen him?" he said after a few moments. She looked over at him sharply. "Absolutely *flattened* him on the pitch earlier- not that that's new..." Luke lifted his shoulders, turned his knees into the aisle towards her and spoke quietly. "Reckons he's not sleeping, but like, as if. Coursework, swimming squad *and* working on weekends? I'd be drooling on my biology textbook before lunchtime."

"Just because nothing ever stresses you out-"

"That's what I'm getting at. I'm just thinking..." he lowered his voice covertly. "Remember year nine when he fucking lost it?"

"Stop it."

The words came out sharply and Ziggy glared at him. He blinked, held up his hands and turned forwards in his seat again.

Silence settled. Ziggy stared out of the window and seethed. At Luke, at Lena, at Jamie. Even at Callum, who hadn't even *been there* in year nine when, as far she remembered, they all lost it.

As the bus neared the village, she glanced over to find Luke playing *Snake* on his phone.

"It must be really nice," she muttered, not really intending to say it aloud. "To be able to just pretend."

Luke crashed the pixelated snake into a wall and looked up, perplexed.

"Eh?"

She shook her head.

"Never mind."

When the bus stopped at the corner shop, she stepped off with a dozen or so others. She stood under the bus shelter out of the rain, waiting for Jamie. Lena passed her with another soft smile. Ziggy didn't smile back.

Jamie was the last one to come down the steps and if her face reflected her mood after talking to Luke for one short bus ride, then his expression shouldn't have surprised her, since he shared two classes with Motormouth Luke.

"Hi," she said, trying not to frown. Failing.

"Hi."

"You alright?"

He didn't answer that. He came under the bus shelter and leaned against the metal seat next to her. She half wished she had Skittles to offer, then bitterly wished she never had.

"I, uh, wanted to ask you about your painting."

"My... which one?"

"The scary one," his lip twitched ironically. "I just wondered if it was, like, from a story or something? Like how you used to draw..." She looked at him sharply and saw him swallow. "...Them."

The word hung between them like a sword for a moment.

"No," replied Ziggy coldly, standing up. "It's from my imagination. Same as everything I *ever* drew."

She didn't look back to see his reaction, and she ignored him calling her name as she walked away, into the damp grey afternoon.

Chapter 11

Ziggy had barely slept. She'd sat up for hours in her room drawing the antlered man again. The fierce eyes, the wet moss. Fur. Blood.

Was he one of Nana Peg's stories? Like the children under the hill and the apple tree? Not that she could remember.

But they had been real. Hadn't they?

She tore out the sheet and crumpled it into a ball, frustrated. Her eyes were stinging, and she gave up.

After that, she'd lain rigid for hours, Puck purring on her chest, listening to the rain on the trees. Once, long after midnight, she'd been certain she heard it outside her window. Not the foxes that barked in the hedgerows, not wind; something pacing. Heavy, scraping. Like it had claws.

When she finally drifted off, the antlered man was waiting for her. In her dream, he wore a sly smile. Pale eyes that cut through the darkness of the trees, seeking out his prey. He stroked the head of his wolf like a friend.

When she woke up, her sketchbook lay open on her desk, the image from her dream there in bold ink, as though summoned by her subconscious. *Or the other way around.*

Ziggy got ready for school with a knot in her stomach.

* * *

Callum was already in the art room when she arrived that morning, bent low over a pencil drawing of a brick wall. It was literally just a brick wall. Ziggy had seen him work on this particular drawing, on and off for weeks and didn't understand how he kept coming back to it, somehow finding more detail to add. Some areas had been worked and reworked so much that the paper was starting to wear thin, but it was so realistic now that she thought it might hold up the roof.

Everyone else was taking their seats and unpacking their work but from the way he sat, one foot underneath him, leaning on an elbow, eyes laser-focused, he might have been there hours already. Ziggy took her usual seat opposite him.

"Was starting to think you moved back to Mordor," she said.

Callum didn't look up.

"Better luck next time."

Miss Tucker had switched on the projector screen and started talking about symbolism and interpretation again. There were a few groans from around the room.

"Alright, well if you all know this, why did three of you come to me last week panicking that you *still* don't know what to write in your analysis essay? You've been doing this stuff for two years. You know your topic. Link it to your work." She looked around in exasperation at several blank faces, a few more anxious faces, and some, like Callum, who weren't even paying attention. "Back to basics it is then!" she exclaimed. "Who remembers our friend Fuseli?"

"Isn't that a type of pasta?" somebody snorted. Nobody laughed.

An image of *The Nightmare* appeared on the projector screen.

Ziggy leaned on her elbow, tilting her head to examine the picture.

"People were fascinated by this painting in the 18th century. Supposedly it was inspired by the idea of an incubus-" Miss Tucker held up her hands, preempting a reaction. "Yes, it's a sex demon. And a lot of you in this room are actual adults now," she breezed past it. "But Fuseli was deliberately ambiguous. Was it literal? A projection of fear or lust? A metaphor for something darker in his mind? We don't always have to have an exact answer… But we need some idea. Here's an easy one…"

The next image on the screen was Van Gogh's *Starry Night.* Six months ago, it may have prompted a lively debate, but weariness and exam anxiety had set in. When Miss Tucker asked if anyone could offer one of the many themes and interpretations of the painting, Callum's pencil scratching seemed to get even louder. The steadily more aggravated teacher was forced to reel off a list of answers herself. Ziggy started fiddling with her pens too. Miss Tucker sighed heavily.

"Okay… For those of you still dragging your knuckles, how about symbolism… The Gundestrup Cauldron. It's from around about a hundred years BC."

She turned to the next slide, showing several images of the massive, elaborately decorated silver vessel. "Have a look at this little chap here, with the antlers…" Ziggy looked up, frowning. "We don't know exactly who this is. It's probably Cernunnos, a Celtic God of nature. Do we think that the artist who made this piece was trying to convey some sort of meaning? Is it telling a story?" she didn't wait for an answer this time. "Probably. But it's also, very simply depicting something that was important to them as a culture and as a human being…" Miss Tucker looked defeated. "A bit like your watercolour rabbit, Becky."

Ziggy stared at the carved silver figure, cross-legged and surrounded by beasts. She wrote *Cernunnos* on the back of her hand.

Miss Tucker was in a mood now and wanted them all to work on their analysis. She even made Callum stop scribbling and reminded Ziggy that she hadn't even seen her final portfolio piece yet.

"It's fine if it's not ready, just bring it in so I can see where you're at with it."

The thought of cramming the wolf and skeleton into her portfolio case on the bus made her sweat, but she nodded.

There was chatter around the room as people bounced ideas off each other and put pen to paper about what their own artistic creations really symbolized and how it linked to the topic, *Time and Memories*.

Ziggy knew what her painting meant. She felt it in her bones, but she couldn't put those words down.

She wrote some brief notes about nature, primal fear and then tentatively wrote *childhood?*

She stared at the word for a long time. She could blag her way through an essay, it wasn't that hard. What really bothered her was the antlered man. She thought about speaking to Callum about it, but he still hadn't even looked at her and then five minutes before the bell rang, a member of staff she recognised from the school office arrived to collect him.

Miss Tucker raised her eyebrows knowingly and Callum followed the woman out of the door with a scowl. Ziggy heard her chuckle as the door closed.

"You're not in *trouble...*"

* * *

Nobody spoke to Ziggy on the bus that afternoon. She rested her head against the cold window to feel its vibration and closed her stinging eyes.

She had sat with Felicity for an hour in the library during a free period that afternoon, working on their essays. Jamie had walked in, looking worse still than yesterday. He stopped at their table.

"Ziggy…"

She raised her eyes, but only as high as his hand, fiddling with the strap of his bag.

"I'm actually really busy," she said. "Unless you've got more art questions."

"No," he mumbled. "Nevermind. See you around."

Felicity raised her eyebrows as he walked away.

"Brrr." She pretended to shudder. Ziggy went back to her essay. "I thought you and him used to be like, besties?"

"*Used* to."

"What happened?" Ziggy eyed her cautiously, and Felicity smiled. "You can tell me. Isn't it ancient history, anyway? Come on, don't make me *Trisha* it out of you."

Hesitating, Ziggy clicked her pen, then she let out a sigh.

"Lena Meyer," she said. It made her chest ache to think about how stupid it all was. "Not on purpose, really… she kind of… grew apart from us after her brother died. We argued a bit and Jamie took her side. I think he always fancied her," a small laugh escaped her at how petty that sounded. "We were still friends though, for a while. It wasn't any one thing."

"Oh. That's boring," said Felicity.

Ziggy laughed.

"I know."

The bus drove over a pothole and a vision of the antlered man flashed through her mind, eyes alive with burning laughter. She flinched, catching a sharp breath. The rain had started again.

Chapter 12

Ziggy came down the stairs just after nine o'clock to make a cup of tea. Piles of books still cluttered the table, but her mother had migrated to the sofa in front of the TV, slippered feet up on the low coffee table. There were books stacked on that too. The news was showing footage from outside a courtroom and June yawned. She turned her head when the kettle started boiling.

"Oh, make us one too, would you?"

"Dad?"

"No thanks, Teeny, but you can pass me the remote. I'm not listening to them go on about the bloody *Coughing Major* anymore. Throw the book at him and move on."

June snorted.

"Oh, be quiet. Don't pretend you never cheated on a pub quiz."

"Excuse me, I'm a strategist, not a cheater!" Gary grinned.

"Strategist, my arse."

Meanwhile, Ziggy had taken out five different mugs, wiped them with a tea towel, put them back, selected different ones and was now rummaging through the cutlery drawer.

"Are you alright, love?" asked June. "This is the third time you've been down to rearrange the cupboards."

"I'm fine, just procrastinating on my Jane Eyre revision. Also trying to avoid texting this boy in my art class again about the essay. Don't want him to think I fancy him."

"Do you?" Gary grinned.

"Dad." Ziggy deadpanned, pouring the boiling water. "You'd love him, actually. Very wholesome type. Extremely shiny bike, definitely never cheated on a quiz."

Her parents both chuckled warmly and Ziggy felt a smile pull at her lips too, surprised at herself for having shared this tiny sliver of information with them and even more surprised that it felt safe.

"Well, if you need something to do besides wear out the carpet on the stairs, you can pop over to Nana's house for me," said Gary, stretching languidly.

June shook her head.

"It's already dark..."

"She's a big girl. She'll be out on her own in a few months."

"What for?" asked Ziggy.

"The estate agent wants to take pictures in the morning. There's a few boxes left out in the kitchen and the bedroom, maybe you could just stick them in the cupboard. Make sure the toilet seat is down, that sort of thing? I don't have time; he's already got a key and he'll be there first thing."

"I should have made the effort earlier," said June, looking around at the books on the table.

"It's alright, I was going to go... but then I sat down, didn't I?" Gary smiled and gave another one of his exaggerated stretches. "You'll nip over, won't you Justine?"

"Yeah, it's fine. I'll just have my tea. It's not raining anymore."

She blew across the top of her mug and looked out of the window. It *was* dark. But the moon was bright, and the sky was clearing. "Maybe it'll be nice tomorrow..."

* * *

The pavements were slick, and the air was damp, but it wasn't too cold. Ziggy wore the hood of her jumper up over her hair and her hands stuffed deep in the front pocket. During the day, she would hardly go anywhere without music playing in her ears, but now she listened to the sounds of the night.

The trees rustled in the faint spring breeze, dripping occasionally. Cars and lorries rumbled by on the main road, and at one point a train whistled out on the field by the apple tree, where Ziggy used to go walking with her friends. When she still had friends.

Stars crept between the clouds, silent sentinels in the inky sky. Ziggy felt strangely observed as she made her way across the road through the village.

Nana Peg's little bungalow was at the end of a long street, one of the last ones at the edge of the village before the pavement turned into a gravel footpath leading out to the train tracks and the fields beyond the old apple tree. During the daylight hours, the street would have been alive with pensioners busily tending their gardens or gossiping over fences but seemed eerily empty in the dark. One of the streetlamps was out, and for a moment she wondered if she'd made a mistake coming here alone. She loved the quiet, but now it felt like something was waiting in it.

Somewhere, a dog barked sharply, then fell silent again. She kept walking, but her footsteps felt too loud now. As she neared Nana Peg's house, she realised they weren't her footsteps.

Someone was running up the street behind her.

CHAPTER 12

"Ziggy!"

She spun around in alarm. Her breath caught at the sight of Jamie, wild-eyed with panic. "Run!" he shouted hoarsely.

"What?"

"Go! It's coming!"

"Wha-"

Her words cut off as Jamie grabbed her arm. She twisted to look over her shoulder, but he yanked her forward.

"We need- to get indoors..."

Ziggy found the key to Nana Peg's house in her pocket and sprinted up the path, skirting the lavender bush, which brushed her legs wetly.

The security light came on as she fumbled the key into the door.

"Come on come on," Jamie panted.

The door opened, and she tripped as he shoved her inside, clumsy in his urgency. He slammed the door and locked it, then stood with his back against it.

They stood in the dark kitchen, breathless. Ziggy backed away, heart hammering.

"What the hell?" she hoped the fact that she sounded annoyed would hide how unsteady her voice was.

Jamie didn't answer. She went to turn on the light. When she saw him properly, her chest tightened.

She'd seen that expression on his face before.

He was pale with fright, eyes locked on the linoleum tiles, both hands squeezing the straps on his backpack so tightly his knuckles had gone white. His hair was damp, and he wore a swimming club hoodie and shorts.

There was blood running down his leg.

"Jamie, your leg. What happened?" she asked, more softly.

He seemed to realise where he was for the first time then, looking around the room as though unsure how he'd got there. Then he looked down at his leg, winced and swore.

"Did you see it?"

"See what?"

"The wolf! The massive… thing!"

"I didn't see anything. Are you okay? Sit down a minute, let me get a towel or something."

Now that he was aware of the blood, Jamie moved much more carefully as he crossed the room and pulled out a chair at Peg's dining table. Ziggy went to the sink, grabbed the towel that hung there and passed it to him.

A four-inch gash tore the back of his leg, just below his knee. The flesh was slashed as though by claws, and blood ran down his calf, staining his sock. His hands trembled as he squeezed the towel around the wound.

"I knew it was following me from the churchyard, but I couldn't see it until it was on me," he said, voice shaking. "It's been following me for weeks, though."

"I heard a dog in the churchyard the other day, too," she said gently.

Jamie looked up.

"It's not a dog."

He hesitated, swallowed. Ziggy thought he might be about to vomit. "Ziggy, it's your painting."

His grey eyes were unblinking and wide. He lifted his glasses to rub them with one hand, while still squeezing his leg with the other.

"I…" Ziggy grappled for words. "What?"

"Your painting," he repeated, wincing. "The wolf. It's been following me. Since before you showed it to me. I've seen it in the hedges around the village. In my dreams… I know it doesn't make sense."

Ziggy's legs went numb. She dropped onto the chair opposite him.

"I feel like I'm going crazy," Jamie said bitterly. "But then I think about what happened… before- with Lena and Nicky. I wanted to talk to you about it…"

Ziggy remembered sitting at this very same table four years ago with two broken ribs. The pair of them took refuge in this house then too. They told the grown-ups she'd fallen from a tree. Jamie had been bleeding from the back of his head, but he never said a word about that. She fiddled anxiously with her locket.

"You're not crazy," she told him. "I've seen it too. I've dreamt about it."

She wasn't sure if the look on his face was relief or fear.

"What is it though?" he asked desperately. Accusingly.

"I'm not sure."

"*You* drew it!"

"It's not…" she clenched her fists in exasperation, her throat was tight against the words but she forced them out. "I didn't do this."

But what if she did?

"Why did it chase me this way then?" he demanded. "Towards your grandmother's house, where you just *happened* to be? It was like it was herding me!"

"I don't know!"

Her voice came out sharper than she meant it. Jamie blinked.

"Sorry," he said. "I'm just really freaked out. I'm glad I ran into you."

Ziggy tried to soften her expression.

"It's alright. I'm glad you're not dog food. Do you think it needs stitches?"

He loosened the towel to inspect the wound. It was angry and ragged but not as deep as it had appeared at first.

"No, it's not bleeding too bad," he said. "I'll sort it out at home. First aid training finally paying off."

"Do you think it's still out there?"

They both lifted their eyes to the dark window. The moon was visible as another cloud parted to reveal its glowing silver face.

"I don't know," he said. "I don't want to go back out there."

Ziggy scanned the little kitchen. The box her dad mentioned sat on the side. A few familiar touches remained, left to give the place a cosy, lived-in look for the estate agent's photos. A tablecloth, a kettle. A tea towel now soaking up blood on Jamie's leg...

"Give me a minute," she told him. "I've got an idea."

Leaving him in the kitchen, Ziggy dashed around the house, making sure the bed was neat, the toilet seat was down and there was no clutter in sight. Once she was satisfied, she grabbed a poker from the metal stand by the fireplace and went back to the kitchen.

"It's made of iron," she told him, holding it like a sword. "Remember?"

Chapter 13

Jamie was pale-faced and limping when he arrived at the bus stop the next morning. Ziggy caught his eye across the crowd waiting there and offered a sympathetic smile.

"Jim-Jam! I'm not gonna make you cry on the pitch again, I swear!" Luke jibed. "You don't need to fake an injury."

"Got bit by a dog, mate," Jamie replied weakly. "Going for a tetanus injection later."

"For real?"

"Seriously."

Luke just raised his eyebrows in surprise and Jamie hobbled over to stand near Ziggy.

"You alright?" she asked in an undertone.

"Yeah…" he answered slowly, uncertain. "Didn't sleep very well though. Kept thinking it was going to crash through my bedroom window."

"Me too," she nodded.

They'd seen no sign of the beast as they made their way back through the village after leaving Nana Peg's house the night before. Ziggy held the poker out in front of them, brandishing it inexpertly but earnestly, her heart hammering in her ribs. They reached her house first, and she offered it to Jamie to take home. He leaned on it like a crutch and limped off into the dark, murmuring thanks and promising to talk in the morning.

"I still don't know what to make of it," he murmured. "I know what I saw. It wasn't a dog."

"I believe you."

He took a deep breath.

"I almost wish you didn't."

The bus pulled up, and they hung back, letting the rest of the crowd get on first. Ziggy took a seat near the middle and was surprised when Jamie lowered himself into the one across the aisle, carefully adjusting his bad leg.

Lena was in the row ahead, leaning against the window, the morning sun catching in her fringe. She turned her head and smiled. But there was sadness in her eyes. Ziggy smiled back.

"Hi, Lena."

Lena didn't speak, but she raised her hand to the back of her seat. Ziggy reached out and touched her fingertips; warm, familiar, fleeting. She looked over at Jamie, who watched silently and although he looked tired and unwell, he smiled too.

***

"Oi! Zinc Oxide Barbie!"

Callum's bike wheels skidded on the pavement as he braked sharply and then slowed down to ride beside her through the school gates. "Wanna hear something weird? That old apple tree we were talking about got chopped down."

"What did you just call me?" Ziggy frowned at him and his face fought to maintain neutrality as he turned away to dismount. He rolled his bike into a space in the bike rack with a haphazard swish and then crouched to attach a lock to it.

Ziggy didn't wait for him. He hadn't spoken to her, apart from a stupid text, and a sarcastic comment in Art, since the weekend. He jogged to catch up with her, pockets jangling with loose change or keys.

"Weird innit? I'm guessing that tree's really ancient. You and me just *happen* to have a conversation about it, and then it turns out it's been chopped down?"

Ziggy stopped and turned to study him, peering closely into his eyes. He coughed an uneasy laugh.

"What?"

"Just checking how high you look before Mr Stokes clocks you."

Callum visibly relaxed.

"Nah, I'm good. Don't you think it's strange though? Coincidence."

"I think *you're* strange."

"Aw, thanks."

Ziggy continued walking, still wishing she could ignore him the way he'd ignored her, but she *did* want to know about the tree.

"How do you know it's been chopped down?" she asked. "D'you go there again?"

"Yesterday."

"How come?"

"Just riding my bike," he muttered, looking away. "I just go out sometimes, y'know..." Ziggy just nodded. She didn't know much about Callum's home life, but she was starting to get an idea. "Anyway, I'm going for a smoke before reg..." he said it like it was a question, looking around awkwardly, as though he was being circled by bees, then shrugged. "Alright, See you later."

He disappeared behind the sports building and Ziggy carried on walking.

It wasn't until halfway through registration, when the moment had replayed a dozen times in her head that she realised. He'd been trying to ask her to come with him.

Chapter 14

Ziggy could tell her mother was tired. It wasn't just the way she moved; slower than yesterday, with the tea cupped in both hands like she was stealing warmth. It was the house itself. The dirty dishes still in the sink. The pile of unsorted books on the kitchen table. The shadows under her eyes, soft and grey.

Ziggy filled a bowl of soapy water, letting it overflow a little.

"Mum, there were some books about folklore from Nana's. Are they gone yet?" she asked.

"Hmm?" June looked up from the armchair. "Nothing's gone yet, love. What sort of folklore? I've seen a few."

"Celtic, I think."

"Oh? Is this for your essay?"

"Sort of..." Ziggy focused on scrubbing a teaspoon. She could feel her mother watching her. "I mean yes. I mean- it is, but also just curiosity."

"You're just like her, y'know?"

"What, Nana?" Ziggy smiled. She knew June didn't mean it kindly. "You're going to say I'm obsessed with stories?"

"I was *going* to say you don't give straight answers to straight questions," June said, smiling faintly. "But yes, that too. You do worry me sometimes, Justine."

The suds were cooling. Ziggy rinsed the last mug and set it on the draining board.

"I know, Mum. But you don't need to," she said, even and quiet, back still turned. "I'm getting better. I revise with Felicity. I even talked to Jamie yesterday."

That earned a genuine chuckle.

"And the boy in your art class?" June teased. "The one you absolutely don't fancy?"

"Mum."

"I'm just asking."

"Don't even."

June was still smirking when Ziggy crossed to the coffee table and picked up a book at random. *The Once and Future King.*

"So," June said, shifting under the blanket draped over her lap. "What is it you're looking for? I've actually read a book or two, in case you hadn't noticed."

Ziggy hesitated.

"Cernunnos," she said finally. "Ring any bells? Celtic god, maybe? Antlers. Nature. I think."

June's brow furrowed.

"Hmm. Maybe. I've heard him called a God of the Underworld before."

"What?" Ziggy looked up sharply. "Really?"

"Yeah. I'm sure that's right. Could be a different version." She yawned and sank deeper into the chair. "You should ask your dad, though. He knows more of the old Welsh stuff; that was your Grandpa Gwyn's territory."

Ziggy nodded, chewing on the thought.

"Is he home tonight?"

"Night shift," June murmured, eyes half-closed. "Try not to

wake him in the morning."

Ziggy sat on the arm of the sofa, flipping absent-mindedly through the pages of the book in her lap. The image of sharp teeth rose again in her mind.

She fished her phone from her hoodie pocket and typed a message without thinking too hard.

If ur out on ur bike b careful. Go home b4 dark. Jst trust me.

She stared at it. Then hit send.

* * *

Ziggy was in the churchyard again, in that Halloween dress; the one she'd outgrown years ago, and plastic cape, her back pressed against the church door. It was a dark night, and the air was cold and still.

The beast was there again too. *Prowling.*

She could see it more clearly this time, as its hulking grey form moved around slowly between the headstones. She could smell it. A mossy, wet animal scent, and something else too. Blood. The smell made her gag.

She wanted to move, but her feet were stuck in place, as though rooted to the ground. The beast knew she was there. She could tell by the way it moved gradually closer, as if drawn by the sound of her thudding heart, which grew louder with every step it took.

She was waiting for the pale ghoul to appear in the trees again, to lure the beast away, her eyes darted towards the trees, then back to the beast. But still it came for her. Yellow eyes burning. Twitching muscle, creeping slowly closer.

Hot breath, like rotting meat. Close enough to feel it against her bare legs.

Then it stopped and sniffed the air. Its head whipped around, and Ziggy's eyes followed.

Not the pale ghoul from her painting, but the little boy in the pitiful skeleton costume. Runny nose and smudged face paint, NHS glasses and untied shoelaces. He stood there beneath the yew trees. Small, solemn and alone. Unaware of what was coming.

The beast took off with a scrape of claws and a snarl. Ziggy's chest lurched. She tried to scream at him to run, but her throat was closed.

Her feet came unstuck, and she was able to move. She started to follow the beast towards the trees, hoping to help the boy, but a sound distracted her. A crunching scrape; wheels on gravel. The wolf heard it too and changed its course, tearing back towards the path. Ziggy turned, too late to see the dark shape of a bike disappear out of the churchyard gates, the beast in hot pursuit.

She ran up the path, skidding on the gravel and stopped at the gate, frozen in awe and terror.

It should have been the familiar, tree-lined street where she'd lived her whole life, learned to roller skate, gone trick-or-treating and grazed her knees. It should have been a quiet night-time scene.

Instead, the gate opened up on a summers afternoon.

It was the dirt path that led to the farmland on the other side of the village, near Nana Peg's house. The train tracks and the fields beyond. The place she'd gone walking so many times with her friends. The place where Nicky had died and Lena had become a monster. The place where she and Jamie had gone to try to save them both.

The apple tree stood just before the track, with its twisting grey branches reaching out like grasping fingers, heavy with fat red fruit. The names carved into its bark were still there, like so many ancient scars. A few crumpled sheets of paper lay in the dirt under the tree.

Ziggy hadn't been back here in years, but she knew the place so well, her feet drew her forwards without her even noticing. She stood in the shade of the branches and picked up the piece of paper. It was a pencil sketch of this same tree, and it was signed at the bottom. *Justine Briggs.* She looked up.

A bloody handprint on the grey bark.

Behind her, the crunch of bike wheels on dirt. She spun around in time to watch Callum ride over the train tracks. She wanted to shout after him that he was going the wrong way, but there was a train coming.

It screamed as it tore across the track. She covered her ears, but it was inside her head, the shriek of brakes, the rattle of iron.

It just kept going. Carriage after carriage blurred past like seconds she couldn't get back.

And when it finally ended, he was already gone.

* * *

Ziggy woke up gasping, her pillow damp beneath her cheek. Her phone buzzed violently against the wood of her bedside table. She fumbled it in the dark, heart still caught in the dream. *Jamie.*

"Jamie?" Her voice cracked. "Are you okay?"

"Yeah..." his voice was quiet. "I had a dream. I just... wanted to speak to you."

"Oh."

"I'm sorry I woke you."

"I'm glad you woke me. I was having a nightmare too."

"Yeah?"

Puck, disturbed from her slumber, padded up the bed and nudged at Ziggy's hand with her head, purring loudly.

"They'll say it's exam stress. When's your first one?"

"Next week. Biology. It feels pointless though…" his voice trailed off, and she pictured his head dropping dejectedly, like the little boy in her dream.

"What are you doing in September?" she asked softly.

There was a pause.

"Nothing," he said. "Probably just keep working. I dunno."

Fresh tears sprang into Ziggy's eyes, and she quickly blinked them away, even though he couldn't see them.

"I wish I was doing nothing," she whispered.

Jamie didn't speak for a moment. Ziggy held her breath against the stream of words threatening to tumble out. Puck purred contentedly against her hand.

"You still wish I'd let them take you," said Jamie. "That day by the apple tree… You wanted to go."

She didn't answer right away. She couldn't.

"Sometimes," she said eventually. "But not tonight."

"Good… I'm gonna try to go back to sleep now."

"Okay, me too."

Ziggy put the phone down and wiped her face again. Her hair had stuck to the tears drying there. She stroked Puck's fur for a while, listening to the patter of rain beyond the window.

Nana Peg would have told her that dreams were symbolic of things that your mind was trying to unravel in your sleep. But she also would have told her a story about dreams being prophecies, or tricks. She could almost hear her chuckling.

"Like Porphyro climbing into Madeline's bedroom on the Eve of St Agnes. You'd never fall for that nonsense, would you, Poppet?"

Ziggy sat up and picked up the little china shepherdess from where it sat on her bedside table. She wound it up with a few clicks and set it back on its stand, then turned off the bedside light. The gentle tinkling tune, melancholy but lovely, filled the dim room.

She lay back in the dark and watched the little shepherdess turn, slowly, like the wheels of a bicycle, like a train pulling away, until her eyes drifted closed again.

Chapter 15

The plastic portfolio case leaned against the wall behind her in the sixth form lounge, a silent weight she couldn't stop thinking about. Ziggy was supposed to be revising her *Jane Eyre* notes. Her highlighter hovered over the margins, but the words kept sliding off the page.

That morning, the case had claimed its own seat on the bus, turned sideways to fit. She'd wrestled it up the steps, pretending it wasn't threatening to tip her over. The canvas inside barely weighed a thing. It was the idea of carrying the *wolf* around; of dragging it back into daylight, that felt impossible.

Jamie slid into the row behind her, his eyes flicking to the case like it might bite.

"Feeling better?" she asked.

"Not really," he said, holding up a battered biology textbook.

Ziggy dropped *Jane Eyre* with a sigh and checked her phone again. No reply from Callum. He probably thought her message was stupid. But he hadn't shown up to school, and it bothered her, not knowing if he was just bunking off, or something worse.

A group of girls came in laughing, one of them evidently having just spilled something on herself. Ziggy looked up and

Lena smiled at her. She broke away from the group and left the others to clean up their mess.

"Hi Ziggy."

Ziggy tried to smile, highlighter lid in her mouth. Lena eased slowly onto the seat opposite, like the cushion might spontaneously combust.

"My class did *Jane Eyre* too," she said. "Do you like it?"

Ziggy shook her head. "Prefer Shakespeare."

"Me too, really. But I find this stuff easier."

Lena tucked a blonde lock behind her ear. She pressed her lips together and looked around. "Is that your portfolio? Can I see it?"

"Um... okay."

Ziggy got to her feet and picked up the portfolio case. She sat it on the seat of the chair and opened it. Hesitated. "Why?" she asked. "I mean, I don't mind. I just-"

"I used to really like your pictures."

"Used to."

"Don't be like that. Your stuff's amazing."

Haltingly, fearing now she'd made too much of a show of it, Ziggy slid her painting out of the case.

Lena's smile evaporated.

"Wow," she breathed. "Ziggy, that's... scary." She leaned in a little, studying it. "Not in a bad way. Just... not like anything else."

"I know. I sort of hate it now."

Lena stared at the painting for a long time, her brow furrowed. She didn't appear unnerved by it in the same way that Jamie had, but she contemplated it as though something about it troubled her.

"Is it real?" she asked quietly.

Her brown eyes locked with Ziggy's and there was something raw and painful in them. *Regret*.

Ziggy put the painting away.

"Yes."

* * *

"Who are you looking for?"

Jamie reached out and swapped the bowl of red jelly on his tray with the orange one on Ziggy's while her head was turned towards the door. The thick smell of gravy and floor cleaner, the clatter of trays and the echo of shouted conversations made her wish she'd remembered earphones.

"Callum," she said. "Have you seen him today?"

"Who?"

"She means Paintsniffer," interjected Luke with a grin. "Probably somewhere drawing a dick on a wall."

Ziggy frowned, ignored him, and swapped the jellies back.

"Oh..." said Jamie, picking tomato out of his sandwich. "Why are you looking for him?"

"Just- I texted him- about an art essay. I'm not sure if he's in school today though."

"Haven't smelt him," Luke shrugged.

"You're such an arsehole, Luke," said Ziggy, aiming a stray crust of bread off her sandwich at him.

Luke put a hand to his chest, mock-wounded.

"I'm sorry, I didn't know you two were shagging," he turned his head to Jamie. "That must hurt."

Jamie just rolled his eyes.

"Actually," Luke continued. "I have seen him around the

village a bit lately. I thought he lived in town, but he went past me on his bike when I came back from the shop the other night. Pretty late."

"His brother and sister live on my street," said Jamie, pulling out another tomato. "They're in foster care, I think."

"I didn't know that," Ziggy blinked.

"Yeah. Hannah's a bit younger than my sister, but they used to walk to school together last year before Molly started secondary. I don't remember the boy's name- he's little. Right menace with a Nerf gun."

"Oh."

Jamie put down what was left of his sandwich and looked at Ziggy hopefully.

"Can I have your jelly?" he asked.

"Fine, but only because I feel sorry for you and your bad leg."

Jamie grinned and swapped the plastic bowls again.

"Sweet," said Luke through a mouthful of chips. "I know you think you're too cool, but you should eat with us more often, it's ever so heartwarming."

Ziggy couldn't help but smile at his sarcasm, though the buzz of the room pressed at the edges of her thoughts. Callum still hadn't shown. Something in her stomach felt wrong, and it wasn't the raspberry jelly.

"I'm guessing you're not playing this afternoon?" Luke asked Jamie.

"Nah. I'm behind on theory, anyway."

"Okay, well, I'm going to get into my kit before the changing room gets too packed." Luke stood up with his tray.

"Enjoy all that *Lynx Africa* in a confined space, won't you?" Ziggy offered him a mocking smile, and he mimed pouring water from his cup over her head, before going to clear his tray.

Ziggy was still chuckling to herself when she turned back to Jamie. He was eating the orange jelly with a furrow between his brows.

"Do you regret the trade?" she asked, nodding at his bowl.

He shook his head.

"You *should* hang out with us more often," he said.

"I don't really like it in here," she poked at the red jelly with her spoon. She always brought her own sandwich anyway, since she only liked cheese and pickle, but she wasn't fussy about jelly flavours. "Maybe *you* should hang out with me more often."

Jamie smiled sheepishly and gave a bob of his head that said, '*fair enough*.'

Ziggy poked at her jelly some more.

"Are you going to eat that or play with it?"

"First one then the other," she said, then took a mouthful of the sweet, slippery goo. "So the reason I'm worried about Callum is that I know he's been hanging around near the train tracks. He told me the old apple tree's been cut down."

Jamie's eyebrows shot up.

"When did that happen?"

"Not sure. Me and him heard the wolf last weekend, before it attacked you, and the tree was in my dream last night. Jamie..." she put the bowl down and fixed him with a serious look. "Do you remember that day, when you put your blood on the tree trunk?"

Jamie's face went pale; the spoon paused halfway to his mouth.

"You joked about it being a payment or something, to bring back Lena. What if it really was? What if something's coming to claim the debt?"

Jamie was shaking his head. He put down the spoon.

"Please don't say that, Justine."

Ziggy pushed the jelly aside. She didn't want it anymore.

"I'm sorry," she said. "I wish I hadn't either." Jamie stared at his plate and the hubbub of the canteen rose around them. "We can figure it out though," said Ziggy firmly, meeting his eyes. "We have to."

Chapter 16

Ziggy went down to the caravan in a bad mood. Brushing past a clump of foxgloves, some of which were nearly as tall as her, she slapped them aside irritably as they tickled her arms.

Puck hopped through the long grass at her heels and jumped up on the table, mewing lightly as soon as the door opened, blinking when she slammed it behind her. The little cat chirruped, weaving around among the paintbrushes that scattered the tabletop.

Her father had been too busy tinkering with his motorbike in the garage to listen to her questions about Cernunnos and Celtic mythology. *Status Quo* had been playing on the radio; that should have tipped her off that it wasn't a good time to ask.

She couldn't remember the last time he'd ridden his bike; he'd taken her on it once or twice, just up the road and back, when she was little, but she didn't like the noise.

She remembered seeing photos of her father long-haired and leather jacketed, grinning like a fox. A faded tattoo was now mostly hidden under respectable layers of cotton, but she knew it was there on his left arm. A woman surrounded by flowers, with the face of an owl. She remembered being frightened by it as a child. Frightened, and enchanted. It was hard to reconcile the young rapscallion in the photos with the dry humoured, if slightly dull man her father had become.

"Yeah, I've heard of it. Pass me that wrench- no, the wrench."

She had picked up the wrong one. Gary got up and grabbed it himself.

"I thought it was to do with nature, but Mum said it's the God of the Underworld or something..."

"Two things can be true. I'm going to rev this in a minute, it'll be loud."

"Oh," Ziggy's face fell.

Her father looked at her and smiled, but there was a wistfulness in his eyes.

"Your Nana hated bikes too," he said.

"Will you be long?" she asked. "I really want to ask you about this."

"I don't know, Justine, depends how long it takes to fix."

He said it impatiently, and Ziggy, stung, turned and left the garage, chased out by the roar of the bike engine.

Now she stood in the caravan and seethed.

Nana Peg would have listened.

And she would have known what to do.

When Little Justine lost her first tooth at school sports day; already a horrible day full of shouting and pushing and the smell of sun cream. Amelia Taylor told her she'd have to put it under her pillow for the tooth fairy. Justine was horrified. She cried and Mrs Thorne let her take the pearly little white tooth to her grandmother in the crowd of grown-ups watching the sack race.

"I don't want the tooth fairy to take it," sniffed Justine. "It's mine."

"Of course it is, Poppet."

"But what shall I do with it?"

So, Nana Peg took it home, and that afternoon they dug a hole in her front garden and planted the tooth.

"What on earth are you doing?" asked Gary when he arrived to pick Justine up, finding them up to their wrists in soil, having dug a far bigger hole than was necessary.

Justine displayed a gap-toothed smile, holding up a small weed fork like a trophy.

"What d'you think will grow?" she asked.

Gary laughed, and he got back into his car, disappeared off down the garden centre and came back half an hour later with a small pot of fragrant purple lavender.

"There you go, Teeny," he said. "Your little tooth can help it grow big and strong."

The sound of the motorbike engine at the other end of the garden sputtered and stopped again. Ziggy turned on her stereo. The music, a tinny, fast-paced rock song, was slightly too loud, but it suited her agitation.

Puck watched her with sleepy eyes as she dug through the drawer for a box of charcoal and pulled out a clean sheet of paper, then sat down at the table to draw. She wanted to capture an image she had in her head while it still lingered there; Callum's bike wheels skidding through the dirt by the apple tree.

The charcoal scratched and swirled against the paper-frenetic, angry lines and dark shapes. She worked messily, smudging the page with the heel of her hand. The shapes wouldn't form; the image wouldn't line up the way it did in her head. She added another line. Smudged it. Made it worse.

Frustrated, she pushed it away and picked up her phone. She

typed out another text.

Ru ok?

The music changed to a softer song, and Ziggy reached over to turn it off, not in the mood for gentleness. She could hear the rain on the roof again now. Puck jumped up and went to sit on the windowsill, looking out, suddenly alert.

Ziggy stood up. Her skin prickled. It was still daylight, but the light had shifted; grey and murky, making the caravan feel underwater. She crossed to the window and looked out.

Just grass. The dripping trees. The tall foxgloves.

But Puck growled now, a low rumble in her throat. And then she hissed, making Ziggy jump. She took a nervous step back from the window. Then she noticed something: one of the foxglove stalks was bent. Not broken but bowed, as if something heavy had moved past it.

Her breath was tight, and she reached out to touch the little silver cat, wanting to feel the soft fur under her fingertips, to know she wasn't alone.

Puck was tense and didn't react at her touch, still staring out into the garden, pupils like wide black pools.

"What is it, Puck?" Ziggy whispered.

There was nothing to see.

Gradually, Puck relaxed. She chirruped again and jumped down to the door, asking to be let out. "Safe now?" Ziggy murmured.

She unlatched the door and let the cat slip out into the wet garden. She watched her scamper up the grass, briefly pause to sniff the foxgloves, then continue up towards the house.

Ziggy went back to the table to pack away the charcoals. Her gaze landed on the sketch again and she frowned. It wasn't as bad as she'd thought at first. The shape of the wheel was fairly accurate; the spokes were messily done but that was how she saw the bike in her mind's eye. It was the rough, spiky shapes in the background that troubled her. The parts she had scribbled and smudged at the side of the page.

The back half of the bike, unfinished, and riderless, tore along a dirt track, leaving the stump of a tree behind it.

And in the smudges of charcoal around the tree, a pair of eyes watched it go.

Chapter 17

Callum's bike, with wheels caked in mud, was already in the bike rack when Ziggy arrived at school on Friday morning. Seeing it gave her a jolt of relief; more than she wanted to admit. A bleak grey morning, it was raining heavily and people milled about with hoods up and heads down. She figured he might be smoking behind the sports building, but hurried to registration, anyway.

The corridors were crammed with people trying to get where they were going and out of the rain quickly. Voices pressed around her, and someone's shoulder jolted her into a wall. She stuck her own sharp elbow out in retaliation.

In Art, she wasn't remotely surprised to find Callum stood at Miss Tucker's desk when she came in, chewing a fingernail while the teacher bent over his work speaking quietly, her face serious but kind. Most of Callum's work was unfinished and with only a couple of weeks until the submission date, he must be starting to sweat. He took his seat with a bleak sigh.

Ziggy took out the wolf painting, determined to finish the skeleton this morning. Felicity came up beside her and peered at it curiously.

"Is it a story?" she asked. "I've never heard one about a wolf and a skeleton."

Ziggy was getting tired of that question.

"It's my story, I s'pose."

"I know a story about a wolf," Felicity offered. She parked herself on the stool next to Ziggy like she was about to ask if everyone was sitting comfortably. "In a forest in Zhongshan, he was running from the King's hunting party when he met a scholar," she still stared at the painting, her eyes searching for some sort of meaning. "The scholar took pity on him and hid him in his bag until the King had passed. But when the scholar opened the bag, the wolf said that the scholar still hadn't saved his life, because he was starving... so now the wolf wanted to eat him."

"Of course he did," said Ziggy. She caught Callum's eye; he was listening too, but with a glazed expression. "He's a wolf."

"I'm simplifying it," Felicity protested with a wave of her hand. "The story's about seeing the good in people. The scholar and the wolf end up in a moral debate with an apricot tree and a water buffalo, it's all very lofty and dignified- I don't know what *you're* laughing at-" she scowled at Callum, whose lip was twitching. He held up his hands defensively.

"But the point is-" Felicity turned back to Ziggy with a meaningful look. "Some people aren't worth it."

Ziggy bristled. *Was that a warning, or a dig?* She didn't know what to make of that comment. It sat in her chest like a stone, anyway.

***

The sixth form lounge was deserted at lunch. Ziggy flung her bag over the back of the twill sofa and flopped down after it, limbs heavy. She lay on her back and closed her eyes. Her head swam with brushstrokes and half-finished lines, so many tiny touches. She'd stared at it for so long that the shapes had become meaningless.

It was dim in here compared to the brightly lit art studio and she tried desperately to tune out the sounds of voices echoing down the corridor, the hum of the ceiling lights and an occasional flick, someone turning a page.

"You alright, Ziggy?"

She sat up with a start.

"Jesus! You made me jump!"

Lena was sitting at a table on the other side of the room, blonde head bent low over a book, but she looked up and smiled.

"Sorry."

"It's okay, I didn't see you there. Aren't you having lunch?"

"Not hungry. Stressed I think," said Lena with the practiced smile of someone used to polite lies. "You?"

Ziggy blinked, searching for words that wouldn't come.

"Dunno," she finally muttered.

Lena looked at her for a moment, then back at her book. Her voice, when it came, was quiet.

"You know what Ziggy… you make it hard for people to be nice to you sometimes."

"I- what?"

"I've been trying, y'know." Lena leaned closer to her book. "I don't know if you can tell. Or you can, but you've just decided you don't care. I've been trying for years… But you're not bothered, are you?"

Ziggy shifted uncomfortably in her seat. Lena was still looking at the book on the table in front of her. "You just want to be able to pretend you're the victim and feel sorry for yourself."

"I-" Ziggy blinked. "I'm pretending you didn't change?" her face was starting to feel hot, and she stood up, folding her arms. "That you didn't- turn him against me?"

"That's what you think? That he picked me over you?" Lena's voice was low, and she gave a little ironic laugh. She finally looked up at Ziggy, who immediately looked away. "Seriously, Justine, you're such an idiot sometimes."

She didn't really want to know, but she asked anyway. "What do you mean?"

"He always liked you better," Lena said quietly. "You were cooler. Smarter. You didn't even have to try." She laughed, dryly. "You didn't even care."

She stood up and approached Ziggy, still speaking softly, as though explaining a thunderstorm to a nervous horse.

"I was just Nicky's sister. That's the only reason anybody wanted to be my friend. And then I wasn't that anymore, either."

She shrugged. Her eyes dropped to the floor. "So yeah, maybe I thought I needed Jamie more than you did, because you made out that you never needed anybody or anything, and maybe *I* wasn't the best friend either... But I was fifteen, and I was stupid and sad. People were calling me names about stuff I didn't even do. Tom Knight told everyone I..." She stopped short, the words dying in the air. She folded her arms, mirroring Ziggy, the sofa in between them like a barricade.

Ziggy's face burned. She'd forgotten about Tom and the things he said about Lena. How angry it had made her, and how instead of sticking up for her friend, Ziggy's drawings had made it worse. Jamie tried to pretend none of it had ever happened.

"So, I decided that it was easier to think you were weird than it was to think about what happened. I'm sorry about that. But it's not my fault that you push people away."

Under her folded arms, Ziggy's fists were in balls so tight it hurt. She stared at the wall and nodded; throat closed against any words that might come out.

"I'm sorry, I didn't mean to have a go at you like that," said Lena gently. Ziggy couldn't look at her though. "I was trying to say that I wish things had gone differently. That we were still friends... You and me."

Ziggy managed a strangled nod.

"Me too," she said. "I'm sorry. I'm gonna go."

Her breath came too tight, too fast. Her bag, her legs, the door. She didn't stop until the air hit her lungs, cold and wet. She stood outside in the drizzling rain.

* * *

Callum was there, but not in his usual spot.

He wasn't watching the traffic this time. He was just folded against the sports hall wall, under the narrow shelter of the roof. His arms rested on his knees, head tipped back to the sky, blowing smoke in the air.

Wordlessly, she sat down next to him. He offered her his cigarette, and she shook her head. His right knuckles were grazed, fingernails chewed raw. One thumbnail was stained black with ink. He still wore that childish bracelet. Ziggy realised now it must have come from his sister.

They sat there for a while in silence, just watching the smoke curl in the damp air. Eventually, he spoke.

"You ever feel like your skin is too loud?"

Ziggy smiled wryly.

"Yeah."

"Sorry I didn't answer your texts. It's been kind of…"

"I get it," she said softly. "I was just worried because- this is gonna sound stupid, but… you know that dog in the churchyard? I don't think it was a dog."

Callum shrugged.

"I know."

"You- what?"

She looked at him to see if he was making fun of her again, but he looked like he'd forgotten what fun was.

"I've seen some weird shit lately," he murmured. "And I don't just mean my stepdad." He turned his head to look at her. "We could live here though. You up for it?" He didn't smile.

Ziggy had heard those words before. Once, long ago, when they'd still meant something like adventure.

Her throat felt tight.

"I'm kind of scared," she told him. She put a hand to her locket, feeling its warmth against her palm. Callum didn't say anything. Down on the road below, cars drove past, and, in the distance, a dog barked.

Neither of them moved.

Chapter 18

Gary Briggs always cooked spaghetti bolognese on a Friday night. When Peter and Justine were little, he used to blend the vegetables so that they didn't notice them, and over the years he had adjusted the recipe to their tastes. He was liberal with the paprika, especially when Peter was at home, and tried not to overdo the garlic because Justine didn't like the smell. She liked cheese though, sprinkling it on her dinner like she was casting a spell.

"This is what I'm going to miss the most," she said.

"Hmm," June nodded, twirling spaghetti on her fork. "I don't know what you'll live on in September. Cheese and pickle sandwiches are easy, at least."

The Who were playing on the stereo. It had stopped raining and the sun was coming out again. The evening looked almost like a promise of summer.

"I've been thinking about York," said Ziggy.

When she didn't speak again immediately, her mother shot her father a look.

"Oh?" prompted Gary.

"Yeah. It's a small city. Everything's walkable. Not too far from home. It feels safe… Peter's there."

"It's a good uni," said June. "And I know I'd feel better if I thought Peter was keeping an eye on you. Not that I think you need-"

"I know, Mum."

"Where are your friends going?" asked Gary.

"What a silly question, you know she doesn't have any friends," teased June. "She tells us often enough."

Ziggy rolled her eyes.

"Felicity's got an offer for Liverpool, I think. I'm pretty sure Lena's applied to do journalism somewhere, I'm not sure about anyone else… Jamie didn't apply anywhere."

"That's a shame," said June. "Not surprising though. His mum'd be lost without him; that sister of his is a right handful. What about *not your boyfriend*?"

"No chance."

She wasn't really annoyed by the playful glint in her mother's eye, but shot her a dark look anyway, content to play along with this narrative June had built.

Gary tore off another slice of garlic bread and dipped it in the bolognese sauce.

"I got the bike running today, Teeny," he said. "I was wondering if you fancied coming for a ride after dinner? It's looking like a nice evening."

Ziggy hesitated, and spaghetti slid off her fork.

"I… I dunno."

"I know it's a bit noisy, but I thought it might be fun. I've got some earplugs you can use."

Gary was spooning sauce onto his garlic bread, not looking at her so intently that she could tell he desperately wanted to look at her.

"Actually," she said slowly. "I've been wanting to go out to look at the old apple tree by the train tracks, I heard it got cut down, so I wanted to see and maybe sketch it… But Jamie got attacked by a dog near there the other night, so I was a bit nervous to go by myself…"

"You *want* to go?" her father looked up at her, smiling, and she glanced away quickly, going back to twirling her spaghetti.

"Yeah" she said after a moment. "Let's do it."

* * *

"Are you ready?"

Gary's voice was muffled by his helmet. Ziggy gripped her father's waist. The leather of her mother's old jacket was soft but rubbed uncomfortably against her neck as she nodded, not trusting herself to speak without her voice giving away her nerves.

"Most of the vibration goes to your toes," said Gary. "You get used to it. Tap my shoulder if you want to pull over."

She lifted her thumb.

The engine roared to life beneath them. A pair of alarmed pigeons flapped off from the tree above the driveway and the gravel crunched under the tyre as it began to roll forwards.

Ziggy gripped tighter.

The helmet she wore was tight around her head, compressing the earplugs and softening the sound. Her own heartbeat thudded in her ears, muffled by the helmet and louder than the engine as they pulled out of the driveway. The church bells were ringing, as though underwater.

Little Justine had never liked loud noises. Too crowded by the legs of strangers when she held her mother's hand at the firework display in the village. Too nervous to make shapes in the air with sparklers with those noisy boys from her class,

Nicky Meyer and Jamie Cleary. Too frightened of the bright, open sky to sit on her father's shoulders like her friend Lena, held aloft like a queen, gazing upward in awe.

But Gary had picked up Justine, so anxious and small, on his back like a koala, she buried her face in his damp shoulder and clung, hiding her eyes from the bright, noisy colours.

Ziggy closed her eyes against the blur of houses and trees, gripping her father tightly, trusting the way he used his weight to steer the bike around corners, knowing that she was safe as long as she held him.

She felt the bike slow and opened her eyes. They were outside Nana Peg's house. It was almost unfamiliar, with the curtains open and the lights off in the dim of the evening. Peg should have been watching *Coronation Street* and sipping a cup of *Yorkshire Tea*. The bike slowed to a stop.

"I hate seeing it all dark..." she heard Gary's voice over the rumble of the engine. "I'm just going to check the back." He turned off the engine and dismounted. "One minute."

Ziggy stayed, sphinx-like on the back of the motorbike, watching as Gary jogged up the path to the little bungalow, in the glow of the evening sun.

She felt a chill.

Something else was watching too.

Ziggy could feel eyes on her. Heard a murmured growl. She was frozen on the bike, but her eyes darted about anxiously.

And then Gary reappeared.

The growl faded, and she wasn't sure if it hadn't been in her head, a residue of the vibration, which started again as the engine came back to life.

"You alright?"

She gave a nod, and they took off again.

The road became a gravel path under the trees, and at the end of the path a clearing gave way to the apple tree and the train tracks.

This path knew her footsteps by now. It had once been the route to everything magic and terrible. She had come this way in the dark as a little girl in a Halloween dress, clutching that skittish little skeleton boy by the hand.

Jamie had nearly slipped away that night. After eating an apple from the tree, he almost disappeared with those creatures that lurked there, eyes shining from the void, sharp teeth and claws reaching…

Ziggy squeezed her eyes shut and held her breath as they rode past the tree, the way she had as a child in the back of her parents' car driving through a tunnel, hoping to make it out the other side. She felt the bump of the train tracks under the wheels. When she opened them, it was fields for miles around.

The dirt path that led out to the flood bank was a mile of hedges and trees. Birds took flight at the approaching sound of the bike, and she watched them fly off, startled from nearby fields and branches.

When they reached the incline of the path to the flood bank, Gary brought the bike to a stop at the top and put his foot on the ground. The fence here was brand new and a herd of fat brown cows grazed on the raised embankment.

"This is where the stile used to be," said Ziggy. "Jamie was going to carve our names into it that summer but…"

Her chest felt hollow.

Her father looked back at her over his shoulder.

"Let's go back," she said.

He turned the bike around again and started back towards the village.

Everything looked so lush and green after the rain. Not like that summer four years ago, when this path had been dry and dusty as old bones. She had gone home filthy with sweat and dirt, sticky with sun cream and apple flavour gumballs.

The hedges looked neat now; less wild, less dangerous, but several of the trees looked taller than she remembered them. It seemed such a long way back to the village. Hard to believe she'd walked it without a second thought, back when Jamie and Lena and Nicky kept her company.

Gary slowed the bike as they approached the train tracks. This time, Ziggy kept her eyes open.

There was the stump.

She tapped her father's shoulder and gestured for him to pull over. He stopped the engine, and she climbed off, still feeling the engine's vibrations through her legs. She pulled off the helmet, hair sticking to her cheeks and approached the stump.

"I can't believe it's gone," she breathed.

"I don't know how many times you've drawn this old tree…" Gary murmured sadly. "I swear, it was the first thing you ever drew. You must have been a toddler."

Ziggy crouched and laid a hand on the stump. Squat, black and damp. Bark crumbling away as it turned to rot. Nothing like the living, breathing creature from her memories. She felt like she was looking at a dead body.

"I wonder why they…"

"I think it was to do with the railway," said Gary, taking his helmet off too. "Something about stopping the roots from damaging the tracks. I'm not sure."

Ziggy frowned.

"But they were here first- *It*, I mean. The tree."

"Times change," Gary shrugged.

"Not everything. Some things are meant to last."

Like Nicky. She wanted to say. *Nicky and Lena and Jamie and me. We were meant to last.*

But she didn't.

The sun was starting to set. The tree was gone, along with the bloody handprint Jamie had left on it four years ago. Was that why the wolf was hunting him now?

Was the blood debt finally being collected?

"Dad, what do you know about the God of the Underworld? Cernunnos?"

Gary raised his eyebrows.

"I know about the Welsh version," he said. "Gwyn Ap Nudd. Your granddad always said he was named after him, the silly old sod. It's all the same mythology though, just different names. Gwyn Ap Nudd was the King of the Fair Folk, the ruler of the underworld. The leader of the wild hunt."

"The wild hunt?" Ziggy felt her stomach drop to her toes.

"Yeah, you know," Gary smiled and wiggled his fingers spookily. "Spectral horses, souls of the dead, hounds of hell. Hunting people down and dragging them off to hell on the night of the blood moon. Just your cup of tea."

"Y-yeah," she replied shakily. "That rings a bell... What... what does he look like, d'you know? Gwyn Ap Nudd?"

"Erm... a bit like a God of Hunting and King of the Underworld. Big. Scary. Not someone you'd want to meet on a blood moon," he said with a half-smile. Then, more seriously as he put his helmet back on. "And antlers... He's got antlers."

Ziggy didn't smile back.

Chapter 19

Callum sat balanced on the back of the bench, his grubby trainers on the seat, watching a man throwing a ball for an overexcited Westie on the field and fiddling with a cheap Bic lighter.

He looked completely at ease. Not like Ziggy. She'd had a knot in her gut since she'd got his text asking to meet him at the park that morning.

She hadn't slept well after the conversation with her father.

She dreamed she was running along the dirt track, in that Halloween dress, following a bloody trail to the stile at the flood bank, only to find that there was a brick wall blocking her path.

A brick wall made of paper, sketched in black ink.

"Oi! Paintsniffer!" Ziggy called. Callum looked over and grinned at her approach. "What's going on? I thought something happened!"

"Not yet," he smirked.

She stopped and punched him in the arm; maybe harder than was necessary. "Oh, good. You're in one of *those* moods. What are you doing here?"

He lifted his shoulders.

"Hanging out with you," he said, eyes following the white

dog in the distance, thumb scraping back and forth across the spark wheel of the lighter in his hand.

Ziggy blinked, surprised by his sincerity, and the corner of her mouth twitched into a smile.

Looking pleased with himself, he jumped down from the bench, pocketing the lighter.

"Is there anything to do around here?" he asked.

"Not really."

"You ever fall off those monkey bars?"

"Lots of times."

"Want to get dizzy on the roundabout?"

"What are we? Six?"

"What's that got to do with anything?"

He grinned with a giddy energy that made her wonder if he was high, but she couldn't smell anything on him. He widened his eyes at her in a challenge, and she couldn't help but laugh.

"Alright, but I'm warning you, I'm hardcore." She held up a finger, and he answered with a mock-serious expression.

"I believe you."

Maybe it was because the sun was shining, or maybe his enthusiasm was contagious, but she almost did feel six years old again. She sprinted to the roundabout and crouched on one of the little plastic seats.

"*Don't* go easy on me."

Callum spun the roundabout hard, sending her whirling faster and faster. The breeze whipped her hair, and she laughed, trying to focus on watching him, since he wasn't moving. Then he stepped onto the roundabout too and rode it with her, around and around until it began to slow down. Ziggy stopped it with her foot.

"I'm not dizzy," she insisted, though when she jumped up,

she felt a little wobbly.

She gave the roundabout a few strong pushes but doubted her ability to get it up to the speed that he had. He leaned into the spin, gripping the centre post with a stupid grin on his face. Ziggy ran around with it while pushing a few rotations to get it up to speed, before stepping onto the metal base next to him, laughing as she watched his eyes struggle to stay focused on the middle distance.

All the fear and uncertainty of the past few weeks melted away as the world spun around her, nothing but blurred shapes and colours. She shifted a little closer to him. Callum put a hand on her bare arm.

His unsteady gaze met hers.

"Dizzy yet?" she asked.

"Yeah."

Emboldened and giddy with wild freedom, Ziggy leaned in and kissed him. Callum's arms slipped around her waist as he kissed her back, as though he had been expecting it. Considering how cocky he was, maybe he had. She'd expected cigarettes, but all she smelled was fresh-cut grass and summer. Her head swam.

When she opened her eyes, she found that the roundabout had stopped turning, but the world hadn't.

"Oh my god, I'm gonna throw up!" she exclaimed theatrically.

Callum cackled and leaned backwards, one arm flailing, the other pretending to reach out for her. He toppled backwards over the middle post of the roundabout, in exaggerated slow motion. He landed on his back on the metal base, arms splayed out above his head, looking at the sky. Ziggy laughed so hard it hurt her belly. Silly, unrestrained laughter. She'd forgotten how it felt to laugh like that.

She dropped down to sit beside him, both trying to stop laughing long enough to catch their breath.

"Why'd you do that?" he asked eventually, squinting at her with the sun on his face. He sounded genuinely curious.

"What? Kiss you? 'Cause I wanted to."

"Not because you feel sorry for me?"

"Why should I feel sorry for you? You're not *that* ugly."

Callum laughed again, and to show she meant it, Ziggy bent down to kiss him once more.

"Maybe I do like you a bit," she said.

"Oh, okay... Good. 'Cause I like you quite a lot."

He said it lightly, as though he was still joking around, but his eyes were serious. He picked up her hand and laced his fingers through hers.

"Did you come here a lot when you were little?" he asked.

"Yeah. I don't think there's as many kids in the village anymore though. Hardly anyone comes here now. We used to go out onto the flood banks too; me and Jamie, Lena, Nicky... you would have liked him."

"Yeah?"

"When you asked if there was anything to do around here; Nicky would have had five different ideas," she smiled. "They'd all get you either wet, dirty or in trouble with your parents- or all three. But you'd do it, anyway. And he never let anybody pick on me."

Callum frowned. Like the thought of anyone picking on her didn't make sense.

She watched him turn her hand over in front of his face, using it to block the sun, and pushed the roundabout slowly with her foot. She didn't care that there was nothing to do, she would have sat there next to him all day, but then a voice rang out from behind them.

"Disgusting behaviour! Think of the children!"

Ziggy startled. She turned her head to watch Luke approach. Callum still held her hand.

"Alright gobshite?" she asked, relaxing again.

"No. Jamie's supposed to be coming but he's being an absolute wet blanket. Text him, will you, Briggsy?"

"He literally got attacked by an animal four days ago," said Ziggy.

Luke looked at Callum.

"You any good in goal?"

"No."

"Perfect."

"I'm very comfortable where I am, actually."

"I can see that," Luke grinned.

"Didn't you *just* say you were bored?" Ziggy said.

"Yeah, but then I found something to do," Callum murmured, barely controlling a smirk.

Ziggy snorted.

"Oh, you're so annoying," Luke groaned. "Please let me kick a ball at you."

That earned a laugh from Callum, which must also have been the criteria to convince him, because he sat up.

"Okay."

He got to his feet, his fingers lingered with hers for a moment and he blinked, as though still dizzy, then ambled over onto the grass where Luke was kicking the football up in the air.

Ziggy took out her phone to text Jamie.

Come 2 park. Want 2 talk 2 u

She watched, amused at Luke's growing disappointment with Callum's football skill. It was as mysteriously fleeting as his skill in art and seemed to waver with his enthusiasm.

After a little while, Jamie arrived, not limping, but still walking stiffly.

"Here he is; our brave little soldier," cooed Luke. He groaned as Callum blocked another shot, then immediately lost interest in favour of hanging from the goal post like a monkey bar. "Please, Jay. It's like playing with a toddler."

Jamie shook his head.

"I'm not even going to work today," he indicated his bad leg glumly. He hovered next to the roundabout where Ziggy still sat, idly turning it with her foot. "What's up?" he asked her.

"Have you seen it again?" she asked him quietly. He shook his head again, eyes on the other two boys. "I think I finally understand what's going on," she told him. "I think it's because the tree was cut down. You made a blood oath, remember?"

He looked at her doubtfully. He hadn't done it on purpose. He'd had blood on his hand and left a smear of it on the tree. When they were fourteen. And now the tree was gone.

"A blood sacrifice," he'd said.

"That's not funny," she'd replied.

"Ziggy. Come on."

"No, you come on!" she snapped. "Don't do that again, you know I'm not crazy. You've seen the same things I have. You're the one that said it was my painting."

Jamie chewed on his lip.

"What are you saying to me, Justine?" he asked tetchily.

"I'm saying that something's coming for you, and we've got to stop it. We need to find out when the next blood moon is."

Chapter 20

"We should go out. Anybody else want to go out tonight?"

Luke jabbed a finger into Ziggy's shoulder, though his eyes were on Jamie. They were all sitting on the grass. Luke had given up kicking the football around. Callum lay on his back behind them, knees bent, eyes closed, a cigarette turning to ash between his fingers.

"My first exam is Wednesday. I can't revise anymore. Let's just get wrecked instead."

Jamie looked doubtful. Ziggy wrinkled her nose.

"Ah, come on." Luke tilted his head towards Callum. "*You* must know somewhere they won't check Jamie's ID."

Callum didn't respond. Luke shook his head.

"Why do I feel like this isn't the first time he's passed out in a park? You sure about this one, Zig?"

Ziggy glanced at Callum's knees pointed skyward, reached over and plucked the cigarette from his hand, stubbing it out on the grass.

"You can come to mine," she said softly. "If you bring the drinks. I didn't do anything for my birthday. My parents will be thrilled. They'll think I have friends. Just… say Lena's coming if they ask."

"Invite her," Luke shrugged.

Ziggy gave a small noncommittal nod. Jamie hadn't said a word since they sat down.

"Remember when my dad lit the fire pit that time?" she said, turning to him. "I cleared it out the other week. I want to try boiling my own inks."

He smiled, just a little.

"Shall I bring marshmallows?"

* * *

"Do you know what you're doing?"

"In theory..."

Ziggy leaned over the open book on the table again, as though checking the instructions, though she knew this step was as simple as 'boil the petals in water'. "I'm not convinced it'll work though."

Jamie looked sceptical too as he peered into the bubbling pan of purplish water and floating mulch. There were some sausages spitting on the grill next to the pan, and the smell was just starting to make Ziggy's mouth water.

Callum was perched like a gargoyle with his knees up on the plastic garden chair by the fire. His hand darted out, and he turned a sausage over on the grill with his fingers.

"Oh my god, use the tongs, you animal!" exclaimed Luke.

Callum's answering grin was sheepish, like he'd forgotten he was with company.

He'd come back to the house with Ziggy that afternoon and helped her drag the plastic garden table out of the garage, briefly stopping to admire Gary's motorbike.

"Are your parents... like, cool?" he asked.

Ziggy laughed.

When her mother appeared at the back door later, he didn't *hide* exactly but found a reason to duck inside the caravan.

"What are you up to?" asked June.

"Is it alright if a few of my friends come over later? We were going to have some drinks and toast some marshmallows before exams start."

June smiled, but she quirked a suspicious eyebrow towards the caravan. "I don't know that one."

"That's Callum."

June paused expectantly, but Ziggy wasn't about to offer anything more.

"I found that book you wanted," she said, holding out the large hardback. It had a design of knot symbols on the front. *Celtic Mythology*. Ziggy took it and tucked it under her arm. It sat now on the table, underneath a bottle of *HP Sauce* and an open packet of bread rolls. There was a box of cider next to it that Luke had brought over, too.

Callum got up, shifted his chair closer to where Ziggy stood, away from the fire. She had a stalk of foxgloves in her hand.

"I'm gonna bring my intrusive thoughts over to you instead," he said quietly, sitting back down.

"D'you think it needs more?" she asked, looking at the petals.

"It looks pretty purple already… Aren't foxgloves poisonous? Like, *stop your heart* or some shit poisonous?"

"Let's not drink it then."

"You might have to remind me."

She laughed a little. He leaned forwards to hug her at the waist. She lowered her chin to the top of his head, eyeing the other boys.

"They think you're weird," she murmured.

"They don't know shit," he laughed. "I'm not weird, I'm limited edition."

Ziggy shoved him away lightly.

"You ever think maybe *you* don't know shit? You can make yourself useful, though. Here, gimme a hand." She ducked inside the caravan and gathering up a few glass jars, directed him to pick up a plastic funnel and some coffee filters. Puck, who had been sleeping on a chair, jumped up and followed them out with a chirrup.

Back by the fire most of the way through his second can of cider, Luke was putting a sausage inside a bread roll. *Using tongs.* He clicked them at Callum like a crab.

"You strike me as a brown sauce man," he said, as though it was a diagnosis.

Callum took a sausage in onc hand and held the funnel steady with the other. Ziggy poured the hot purple mixture from the pan.

Once all the petals were gone, she poured the ink back into the pan to reduce and added a few drops of thickening agent.

"Don't forget the eye of newt," Callum grinned over his drink.

"I'm doing the lavender next," she replied with a smile. "From my Nana's garden. Grown from my very own baby teeth. Spooky enough for you?"

She caught Jamie's eye, and her smile died on her lips. He had been quietly watching the flames, laughing along at Luke's jokes and complaining about Ziggy's CD collection. Now, in the fading light, the shadows flickering on his face made him look deathly pale.

"Justine!"

She startled at the sound of her father's voice calling from the house, then handed the wooden spoon she was using to stir the thickening agent into the ink to Callum.

"Don't let it burn," she told him, before turning to head up to the house.

There was a coolness in the spring air now, and the long grass tickled her bare ankles, but it wasn't cold.

Lena stood in the doorway with Gary. She was wearing a strappy top and jeans. Her feathered earrings seemed almost a part of her loose golden hair. She would have looked more at home in a *Saltrock* advert than stood there in the Briggs' kitchen.

"Look who's here," Gary smiled. "Just like old times."

Lena hadn't responded to her text message, and so Ziggy hadn't expected her to come.

Lena's smile was weak, and neither of them could quite meet the other's eye, but Ziggy's father filled the silence before it could become awkward.

"Perfect timing Lena. I don't think anything's burnt yet except a couple of fingers. Have fun, girls."

Lena followed Ziggy down the garden and suddenly her face lit up in a smile. A real one.

"Remember when Nicky climbed that tree?" she pointed to a tall silver birch. "Stripped down to his pants and pretended to be *Tarzan*?"

Ziggy laughed.

"I remember being called Jane for a week in year two," she said. Then, after a pause. "What do you reckon he'd be doing now?"

Lena looked around, at Jamie sipping his cider and Luke poking a sausage on the fire. She shrugged.

"This."

She hadn't meant it like that, but Ziggy smiled.

"I'm really glad you came, Lena. I'm sorry about yesterday."

"Me too."

Luke, overhearing this as they approached, handed Lena a can of cider.

"Briggsy, am I the only person here you don't have a complicated relationship with?" he grinned.

"It's not complicated with him." Jamie murmured, briefly nodding at Callum before looking back down at the Celtic mythology book that was now in his lap. He was studying a page Ziggy had bookmarked with a sprig of lavender.

"Nah," agreed Luke. "Just weird and ill-advised."

Ziggy punched him in the arm and went back to take the wooden spoon from Callum, who as usual seemed unbothered by whatever comments were being made about him. Puck was weaving around his ankles, and he crouched to rub behind her ears.

"What's that?" Lena was asking Jamie.

He read from the book with a voice like dry leaves.

"The wild hunt is a supernatural cavalcade of riders and hounds that comes from the sky and roams the countryside…" he shifted in his seat.

"The hunt…" He looked up at Ziggy, frowning, and she turned to pick up the pan of ink. She began pouring into a jar, avoiding his gaze. "Chase and hunt souls… to take them to the Underworld… In Germanic folklore the hunt is often lead by Odin, but in Celtic tradition, it may be led by figures such as Cernunnos, the God of Nature, or the Welsh King of the fair folk, Gwyn… Ap Nud-"

"Gwyn Ap *Neeth*…" Ziggy corrected his pronunciation, without turning around. She was holding her breath. The fire crackled. Callum looked up at her expectantly, while the cat rubbed herself against his hand.

"The wild hunt is often associated with winter months," Jamie continued. "But also, during a solstice, or a lunar event such as a blood moon…when the boundaries between worlds are believed to be thin."

"Is this research for your painting?" Lena asked. She had pulled up a plastic garden chair next to Jamie and was sipping her cider, but she looked troubled. "The wolf chasing the skeleton? Kind of sounds like a hound hunting a lost soul…"

"Kind of," Ziggy agreed.

"Kind of sounds like Jamie coming back from the swimming pool the other night, too," said Luke. He let out a burp. "D'you want a sausage, Lena? I'm burning this one special."

Lena didn't answer. Ziggy still didn't turn around. She was still looking at Callum; those slightly too widely spaced eyes of his were locked on hers. He gave the tiniest nod.

"Am I drunk or are you all acting *really* weird?" asked Luke.

Ziggy turned around. Lena had a hand on Jamie's arm and was staring at a page in the book, her face drained of colour.

"I've seen him," she whispered.

Ziggy hesitated. She glanced back at Callum again and he raised his shoulders as though it was all incredibly obvious. She moved in closer to the picture. She already knew what it was, but she had to see it, anyway.

Of course, it was the man with the antlers, dressed in moss and fur. Cernunnos. Gwyn Ap Nudd.

"I drew him," said Ziggy quietly. "I've dreamed about him. Jamie has too."

"No. I saw him," said Lena. "Under the hill, four years ago."

Chapter 21

Ziggy shivered. The night was growing colder and smoke from the barbecue curled through the air. The shadows of the garden had grown longer. Jamie closed the book with a slap, like he could trap the image of the antlered king of the underworld inside it.

"Would toasting marshmallows right now ruin the drama?" asked Luke.

Nobody said anything, but Callum got to his feet and joined him at the fire, skewering a couple of pink squashy marshmallows on the metal prongs Ziggy had found in the kitchen that afternoon.

Lena's hand lingered on Jamie's arm. They shared a look that Ziggy couldn't decipher, and his shoulders relaxed a little.

"What's a blood moon?" he asked.

"A total eclipse of the moon," said Luke. "There's one on Tuesday. The sun's in Taurus; the moon's in Libra. Mercury's in retrograde too, so maybe that's why we're all fucked..." Everyone was gawking at him. His face flushed, and he turned away, skewering another marshmallow. "You know my mum's mad about that shit."

"So that's when I get dragged off to hell?" asked Jamie, deadpan. "Fun."

"Will you still have to sit your exams?" wondered Callum.

He picked up a marshmallow from the grill and held it out to Jamie as if it might help. Jamie squinted at him sceptically, but then he huffed a laugh and accepted the skewer.

Lena got up to change the music.

Pleased with how rich the foxglove purple had come out, Ziggy began preparing the lavender she had ready to make ink, picking the tiny petals off the stalks. She needed to keep her hands busy. There was a dull queasiness in her gut that had less to do with the cider and more the creeping unease that everything about this night suddenly felt strange and wrong.

She rubbed the petals between her fingertips, already stained purple, like bruises.

Callum came over with a marshmallow still on fire. She was slightly alarmed at how quickly he put it in his mouth after the flame died down, but he didn't flinch.

"Smells like…" he frowned thoughtfully.

"Your insides burning?"

"I mean that," he nodded at the lavender.

"Smells like my Nana. She would not have liked you."

"Smells like…" he tried again.

"What?"

He smiled, like he was trying to remember something but couldn't find the words. He shook his head.

"I dunno. Do you want a marshmallow?"

Ziggy just wished he would keep still for a moment. She reached for his arm, but he was already turning back to the fire.

She sprinkled a handful of squashed lavender into the pan.

"Don't you have anything more upbeat?" Lena asked, discarding a *Queens of the Stone Age* CD. "Your taste in music is almost as depressing as Jamie's new life expectancy."

"Oh, so we *are* making jokes about this," Jamie nodded. He raised his drink in a grim toast. "Cool."

Ziggy went into the caravan for some water to boil the lavender. When she came back out, Lena, Jamie and Luke were racing to finish their drinks. Their laughter floated in the air too easily, like it had no weight. Like none of them remembered what they'd just read in the mythology book.

Callum was frowning at his phone.

"I've gotta go," he said darkly.

"You in trouble?" she asked.

He hesitated, then shrugged. "Maybe. No... I'm not sure." His three different answers came out in varying tones of voice that left her with no clue to the real one. He frowned like he was annoyed at himself, and it occurred to Ziggy for the first time that it wasn't that Callum lied, just that he'd never learned how to tell the truth properly.

She looked up at the sky. The stars were out and the moon, waxing gibbous, was fully visible after weeks of grey skies. The fire was a beacon, and suddenly it seemed dangerous to step away from it. The others would go home soon too, but Jamie was only going around the corner, Lena and Luke could walk together to the other side of the village. Callum had three miles to cycle on his own, in the dark, with a harbinger of the hunt out there somewhere.

She touched his hand.

"I'll be alright," he said softly. "I always am."

For a moment, he seemed about to kiss her, but he thrust a marshmallow skewer into her hand. She gave a weak laugh and followed him towards the house.

"Hang on."

He turned back, nearly stumbling into the foxgloves, and she realised he was almost as drunk as Luke.

She kissed him. This time he did taste like cigarettes. And marshmallows. He pulled away slowly, as if he didn't really want to. Luke wolf whistled at them.

"Just don't get killed or anything stupid like that," she said.

He smiled like someone who'd been given a gift.

"See you."

Callum lifted a hand. He disappeared into the darkness, the shadows swallowing him without a sound, leaving Ziggy with an empty, sick feeling in her stomach. Her hand went to her locket for something to hold on to.

She walked back up the garden, scowling at Luke and Lena, who were giggling and singing, *'Is She Really Going Out With Him?'*

"You all wonder why we stopped being friends?"

"We're just kidding," Lena smiled. "He's alright."

"Yeah," agreed Luke with a shrug. "If you're into woodland creatures. Which I know you are. So, y'know. Happy days."

A laugh escaped Ziggy, despite herself.

Jamie was staring at the flames. The light glinted off something in his hands and she was surprised to see that it was his Swiss Army Knife. He'd had it for his fourteenth birthday and used to take it everywhere, but she hadn't seen it since that strange summer four years ago. He clicked it open and closed distractedly.

"Callum ate an apple from the tree once too, didn't he?" he said quietly.

Ziggy stirred the lavender. She nodded.

"I can tell…" Jamie opened his mouth like he was going to say something else, then shut it.

"What?"

He clicked the knife open. Shut again.

"You don't think he's..." he glanced at Lena.

Ziggy blinked.

One of them.

That's what he had been going to say. The words she didn't want to hear curled in her stomach like a hot chunk of lead.

"No," she said immediately.

The hardness of her expression was enough to make Jamie hold up his hands in defense.

"Okay," he agreed. "I'm sorry."

Feeling her face get hot, Ziggy turned away to carry on with the lavender ink while the others finished their drinks and played a game of Knock Out Whist with a pack of cards Lena found in the caravan.

They had all learned to play one rainy afternoon at Nana Peg's when they were nine years old. Nicky had been prodigious. Jamie couldn't remember the rules. Lena cheated, but only once, and guiltily admitted it immediately.

"Why don't you want to play, Poppet?" Peg asked Little Justine, who cautiously just watched, chewing on a fingernail.

"I want to be on Jamie's team," she whispered.

Ziggy watched them as if through thick glass. She remembered the rules. She remembered Nicky's laugh. She remembered everything that happened after, too.

She poured water on the fire. It hissed and died, steam rising, bringing darkness crashing down on them.

The night was cold. Haunted.

"Can we go inside?" asked Luke, sounding nervous for the first time.

The lights buzzed inside the caravan, he examined the

sketches on the walls, strangely quiet. Puck had followed them inside and hopped up on the windowsill, looking out into the garden with ears pricked. Jamie stood beside her and looked out too.

Luke sat down at the little table next to Lena, who was tidying away some of Ziggy's sketchbooks to deal the cards again. Underneath was the charcoal sketch; the bike passing the tree, the eyes glaring from the shadows.

Luke picked it up, frowning.

"Is all this really real?" he asked. He sounded like a child.

Ziggy's eyes were on Jamie when she answered, his gaze focused on the darkness outside.

"Yes."

Puck was crouching low. And then she sprang away from the window, startled, and darted under a chair.

Ziggy's heart thumped. Jamie stepped back from the window suddenly and bumped into her.

"Do you have anything made of iron in here?" he asked on a low breath.

Ziggy shook her head.

Lena had frozen with the deck of cards in her hand.

There was something outside the door. They could hear it breathing. A heavy rasp, like chains across a dirt floor.

"Draw it," Lena said.

"What?"

It was scratching at the door. Sharp claws. Hot breath.

"The things you draw come true!" she hissed. "Draw it leaving us alone!" She shoved some papers across the table, eyes wild.

"I don't think-" Ziggy winced at the sound coming from the door. Jamie had backed away into the cupboard, knocking over a pot of paintbrushes. "It doesn't work like that, I can't just-"

"You don't know how it works!" exclaimed Luke. "Try!"

Gripped by panic, Ziggy's hands were clenched at her sides. They were all looking at her and she didn't know what to do.

She squeezed her eyes shut.

Draw without thinking.

"Give me some papers," she said.

She grabbed at the sheets Lena thrust at her from the table, tossed them on the floor along with a handful of charcoals and crouched to draw.

Quick, furious lines. Straight. Angular. Thoughtless.

The door cracked. A throaty growl. Lena whimpered. Luke peered at the papers.

"What are you-"

"Help me!" she snapped. "Tape- over there." She pointed to a box of stationery on the table and Lena grabbed it.

Fumbling, she tore strips of tape, passed them to Jamie. He stuck them to the papers. With trembling fingers, Ziggy slapped the pages to the door as it rattled in its frame.

The wolf rumbled angrily. She could smell it through the door. Foul and mossy.

The charcoal lines of each sheet of paper joined up on the door to form an image. A brick wall.

Ziggy was breathing fast. The sound of her heart beating was so loud in her ears that it took her a moment to realise that the scratching had stopped.

She looked around at the others. Lena had tangled up tape stuck on one hand and gripped Jamie's arm with the other. He was ashen faced, holding another sheet of paper up like a shield, though it had nothing drawn on it. Luke hadn't moved from behind the table. His knuckles were white on the corner of it.

"Ziggy," he breathed. "I'm sorry if I ever called you weird. You aren't weird, you're fucking terrifying."

The door stood silent. The wall she'd drawn had held.

Chapter 22

Ziggy leaned on her elbow at the kitchen table, staring out of the window at the bleak grey sky, her tea going cold. The wall of sketches was gone. So were the others. She hadn't slept, not really, but the sun had come up, anyway. They'd survived the night.

Her mother lifted another pile of books into a cardboard box.

"A bit worse for wear?" asked June. She nodded at the empty cans of cider that poked out of the top of the recycling box in the corner.

"I only had one," Ziggy replied. "I'm just... tired."

"Is that your social battery done 'til Christmas then?" June smiled.

As if on cue, there was a knock at the door.

"It's Sunday..." June groaned, looked at the clock and sighed an acknowledgment that it was actually nearly lunch time. Tying her dressing gown around herself, she went out to the hall.

Ziggy sipped her tea, regretting letting it go cold. An unfamiliar man's voice spoke to her mother. She sat up straight.

"...seventeen-year-old boy. We'd like to speak to your

daughter."

"Not another one..." June muttered under her breath tiredly, then called, "Justine!"

Ziggy's chair scraped back loudly across the kitchen floor.

Two police officers, a man and a woman, stood on the doorstep in the damp air.

Ziggy hovered at her mother's back. She clutched a handful of the fabric of her dressing gown like a toddler grabbing a teddy bear.

"What is it?" she asked.

"Sorry to turn up unannounced. We're looking for a friend of yours," said the male officer, a walking moustache of a man. "Callum Blake. We understand you may have seen him recently?"

Hesitating, Ziggy looked down at her feet.

A flash of blood-soaked shoe in her mind's eye. Her mother didn't move from in front of her.

She shook her head stiffly.

"Have you heard from him?" The woman took over, using a reassuring tone. "He's not in trouble; we're just a bit worried about him."

"Why? What's happened?" asked June.

The officers exchanged a look, and the man spoke carefully.

"An accident, this morning. A car knocked him off his bike near his house, but he got back on and rode off in a hurry. The driver of the car reported it."

Ziggy almost felt relieved. They weren't here because Callum or Jamie had been torn apart by a hellhound. *Not yet anyway*.

"His mum hasn't turned up yet, and stepdad's in custody; drugs charges, parole violation. A neighbour heard a disturbance, and it was clear when we knocked on the door something had happened at the house this morning. We think Callum was probably running away again, but he might be hurt."

"Does he have a dad?" asked June.

"Lives in Scotland, apparently."

Ziggy's throat was tight. She could feel her mother's eyes on her.

"He's not with his brother and sister's foster family, but their neighbour said you're his girlfriend?"

They were looking at her expectantly, but her mouth couldn't form words.

"He was here last night," June said gently. "Justine had a few friends over. They had a barbecue in the garden. She…" she put a gentle hand on Ziggy's arm. "She was friends with Nicholas Meyer. Do you remember that case?"

"Oh-" the officers exchanged a look again. "Yes."

"It's… just a bit of a shock to see you standing on the doorstep."

The man nodded. He offered a kind smile.

"Have you heard from Callum this morning?" he asked.

Ziggy shook her head. She took her phone out of her pocket. She had one new message: from Jamie.

Police looking for paintsniffer. Theyre coming to talk to you.

"Do you mind if I have a look?" asked the officer.

She lifted her shoulders, handed over the phone.

He squinted at the messages from Callum on her screen.

"What does he mean by this?"

least I'll die happy

Ziggy felt her face get suddenly hot.

"He thinks he's funny," her voice came out thin.

"Yes," said the officer, eyebrows going up. "We have met him. Did anything seem off about his behaviour last night? Can you think of anywhere he might go?"

Ziggy's stomach felt hollow. The truth was that she *thought* he would come here. Like that night when they went into the churchyard and heard the wolf. The fact that he hadn't come knocking at her caravan door was more worrying than anything. *Where could he be*? She shook her head slowly.

"No more *off* than usual."

He nodded as though that statement made sense too and looked at the woman with an expression that said they'd run out of ideas.

"You'll let us know if you do hear from him, won't you?"

Ziggy nodded slowly. Then she cleared her throat.

"Is he really not in trouble, or are you just saying that?"

The woman smiled, a little sadly.

"Justine, if you know Callum, you know he's always in trouble, but not in *that* way..."

The police officers left, and June closed the door. She turned to her daughter, who stood there with arms folded across her chest.

Ziggy's nails dug into her palms so hard it hurt. Her mouth stayed a hard line.

"It'll be alright," said June. She wrapped her arms around her, pulling her into the soft flannel of her dressing gown. "I'll bet he's hiding out at a mate's house. A bit bruised, that's all. I saw that bike of his; absolute death trap."

Ziggy nodded into her shoulder, breathing in the scent of fabric softener.

"He really isn't bad," she said, voice cracking. She needed her mother to understand. "He's just one of those people that bad things happen to."

June stroked her hair.

"You're a good thing."

Ziggy wasn't so sure.

Chapter 23

June tried to convince her to come to the secondhand bookshop to drop off the boxes of books 'to keep her mind off things' but she shook her head.

She'd paced restlessly, texted Callum twice. Tried to draw, paced some more.

"I think I'll walk to Jamie's house," she said, grabbing her shoes. Maybe he knew something. Maybe he didn't. Maybe she'd already left it too long. But she had to do *something*.

She left the house, hoodie over her hair in the misty rain, feet itching with impatience. She walked to the churchyard, hovered at the gate, peering around, half hoping, half afraid to see a battered bike on its side in the middle of the path, or leaning haphazardly against a headstone.

The damp stones stood like cold grey sentries, and Ziggy didn't linger. The empty path mocked her. No bike, no sign of anyone. She quickened her pace toward Hobbs Row, each step pushing against a growing dread, and knocked on the front door she knew so well.

Lisa Cleary's face split in a wide smile when she saw Ziggy. She was dressed in cycling shorts and a tee shirt with a picture of Freddie Mercury on the front. Her hair, ash blonde without a single grey, was bundled into a high ponytail.

"I'm so glad you came over, are you okay?" she exclaimed, ushering her into the living room. "I had no idea you knew Hannah and Ollie's brother until Jamie told the police this morning. They're such lovely kids."

She went to the bottom of the stairs and shouted.

"Jamie! Ziggy's here!" She turned to Ziggy, a small crease between her pale eyebrows. "It makes me so annoyed," she said. "Social services took the younger ones but left him because apparently, he was *old enough*. Old enough for what? The times I've seen that boy turn up in the middle of the night..." she stopped herself, then sighed. "Sorry, I just hate seeing kids grow up too fast."

Ziggy nodded. She never knew what to say when adults talked like that. It felt like she was part of something she couldn't see.

The Cleary's little kitchen was just as cluttered as she remembered it. Gone were Molly's childish drawings, stuck to the fridge with alphabet magnets, replaced with family photographs. Pretty blonde Molly doing a peace sign next to a sandcastle at the beach. Adam, tall and unfairly good-looking, dressed up for a wedding, grinning with his arm around whatever girl he happened to be seeing that week. Jamie and Nicky, sitting on the wall outside the primary school on their last day of year six. Nicky was shouting to someone behind the camera, the sun glinted off Jamie's glasses.

Jamie came down the stairs.

"I thought you were going to yoga," he said to his mother.

"I'm off now," she said. "If you're going out, don't forget it's your turn to peel the spuds."

Ziggy stood silently leaning against the kitchen cupboard after Lisa left. Jamie chewed on a thumbnail.

"Callum'll be fine. He's hiding, that's all. He always hides. From his stepdad, from everyone. This is just more of the same." But his voice cracked a little. His fingers twitched against his side. "It's me they're after now."

"He ate an apple, Jamie. You said it- you know... you *know* how hard it is to pull away from that."

For a second, she thought he'd agree with her, maybe nod quietly like he used to when they were little, when only he understood why the world felt like too much sometimes. She wanted that version of Jamie back; the one who never laughed when she needed to repeat things, who didn't ask her to explain why she needed quiet, or certainty, or space.

"If you're seriously going to ask me to go with you to look for your weird boyfriend..." he trailed off when Ziggy took a step back, as though the word "weird" had physically slapped her.

"I can't believe you just said that." She shook her head.

Jamie let out a long breath, looking at the floor.

"Do you understand how scary this is, Justine?"

"Yes, actually," she snapped. "I was there, *Jamie*, same as you."

"And you talk about it like it's a story!" he exclaimed. "Like it's just something that happened, not that you feel any particular way about it. You drew pictures of those things like they were characters in a book, when all Lena and I wanted was to forget about the thing that killed Nicky."

He pressed his lips together, as though belatedly trying to stop the words escaping. Ziggy felt her eyes prickle with tears, and she turned away from him, towards the door. Jamie opened his mouth like he wanted to take it back but said nothing.

"Fine," she said, her voice tight. "I don't need your help. And

I guess you don't need mine, either."

She slammed the front door behind her, scrubbing away angry tears. She stood in the misty rain and squeezed her fists tight, nails digging into her palms.

Why had she come here? Weren't the last four years proof that Jamie wasn't the same person anymore? That she wasn't the same person anymore?

She pulled her hood back up over her hair and started walking. Halfway down the row, something made her stop. She looked up.

A small, dark-haired boy was watching her from the upstairs window two doors down. His face was solemn, his eyes wide and searching, like he was trying to figure out what she was doing.

She raised a hand. A flicker of recognition passed across his face, and he waved.

Ziggy's chest tightened.

The boy turned away from the window, the moment passed, and she kept walking.

* * *

Ziggy sat on the stump of the apple tree, listening to the steady rumble of the approaching train. Her sketchbook was open on her lap, the page marred with jagged lines and meaningless shapes of smudged black ink.

Her heart thudded in time with the rhythmic thrash of metal. Louder still as the train drew nearer. Her breath was ragged. Hot tears spilled down her cheeks.

She tore out the page.

The train screamed past.

Ziggy bit down on her lip. She couldn't do it. She couldn't draw Callum back into the world. Couldn't make Jamie safe. Couldn't make herself normal. She wasn't magic.

Chapter 24

Ziggy brushed the last of the dark shadows around the feet of the skeleton in the woods. The quiet in the art studio was almost oppressive that morning, thick with concentration and the smell of turpentine. Some students whispered over final details; others sat in anxious silence. For many of them, this was their last proper day of school.

Nobody mentioned Callum's absence. Ziggy turned her back on his empty seat.

The painting was finished. Finally.

She stepped back and stared.

The wolf sprang from the canvas, all sinew and bared teeth, its fur a mass of bleeding ink and brushstrokes. It wasn't just snarling. It looked *hungry*.

And in front of it, in the pale red light of the moon, the boy in the skeleton costume. Grief-stricken and alone, hands curled into fists, his face paint smudged by tears. He was running. Away from the wolf, but deeper into the woods.

Ziggy's skin prickled.

It was the best work she'd ever done. She hated it.

But it was finished. And now it was out of her hands.

"Are you alright?"

She startled at Miss Tucker's voice, blinking back tears. She hadn't realised they'd formed.

"It's very powerful," the teacher said carefully. "I can't say I *like* it. But it's... powerful."

Ziggy tried to smile.

"It's about childhood," she murmured. "Getting eaten up by the big bad world. The things we're scared of when we're little... I don't know if it makes sense anymore."

Miss Tucker looked grim.

"That's a common theme," she said softly. Her eyes lingered on the empty space behind them. The sheet of paper with the brick wall sketch lay flat on the desk.

"Your work is phenomenal, Justine. You're going to do so well next year. Whatever you decide to do."

* * *

Leaving the art room, Ziggy caught sight of Felicity about to go through the double door at the end of the corridor.

"Fliss... hey, wait!" she jogged a little to catch up. "Can I... can I come to lunch with you?"

Felicity raised a doubtful eyebrow.

"Why?"

Ziggy blinked.

"I, uh..." she lifted her shoulders. "I dunno. I just thought..."

"I'm meeting Darren in a minute," Felicity shook her head slightly. "I thought you were hanging out with Jamie again?" she pursed her lips in a way that made Ziggy shrink. "It doesn't feel all that great, y'know? To be your second choice. I can do better, actually."

"I- I didn't mean-"

"I know you didn't," she rolled her eyes. "But it's our last week in school. Don't expect me to waste my time waiting for you anymore."

She turned and walked away, leaving Ziggy standing alone, gripping her sketch book tightly to her chest like a life belt, biting the inside of her cheek and wishing she knew the magic words to stop people from walking away from her. She didn't blame Felicity. But it still felt like being gutted with something blunt.

Behind her eyes, the image of the wolf in her painting reared up again, snarling, jaws wide.

Felicity's voice echoed in her mind, low and careful, from that afternoon last week in the art room:

"The wolf said the scholar hadn't saved him, because he was starving... so now he wanted to eat him."

At the time, Ziggy had a feeling that Felicity might have been warning her about Callum. Now... she wondered if the warning had been about her. Or Jamie. Or maybe they were all wolves in the end, just fighting over scraps.

* * *

Ziggy drifted ghostlike through the sixth form lounge where were three girls from her English class were quizzing each other on Shakespeare. The sharpness of Felicity's words still buzzed in her ears.

"I'm actually going to cry if I have to memorise another soliloquy," one of the girls was saying to her friend. She looked up and smiled at Ziggy, maybe an invitation, or maybe not. Ziggy couldn't smile back. Her face didn't work like that today.

The girl quickly turned away. Whispered something to the others. Laughter. Ziggy didn't really care if it was about her or not, but something about it it still made her stomach flip.

She dumped her bag at her usual corner table and sank to her knees. But this time, she didn't unpack her sketchbook, or her lunch. She shoved her earphones in and hit play. The CD span. Her ears filled with screaming guitars.

She covered her face with both hands and wished she could disappear.

Under the table. Into the earth.

She knew she was breathing too heavily. She didn't care that people came in and out of the lounge. She didn't care what they thought. Her throat burned.

"Ziggy..."

The voice was far away at first, and then close, crouched beside her.

She pulled out one earphone. "I'm fine," she said quickly; too quickly. The effort of pretending she wasn't drowning was too heavy a weight.

"Oh, for sure," Lena said dryly. "Obviously. But I just wondered what you're doing this afternoon?"

Ziggy blinked. Her voice didn't come.

"I'm getting out of here," Lena said, standing again, like the moment hadn't happened. "Going over past papers in English for the millionth time is a waste of oxygen. I can do that alone. Thought you might want to come."

She said it like it meant nothing. Like she wasn't throwing Ziggy a rope. Like she hadn't just offered her the tiniest raft in an ocean of noise and teeth.

Ziggy nodded slowly.

Lena flicked her wrist to check her watch. The brown leather one with the old-fashioned brass face. Nicky's watch. "Bus is in ten."

Chapter 25

Lena didn't speak on the bus, but she sat beside Ziggy in the aisle seat and offered her a Polo mint. Ziggy smiled a little as she took one. She sank into her seat and watched the trees and road signs pass by the window in a blur.

It was only when they alighted the bus outside the corner shop on the main street in the village that Lena finally turned to her and spoke.

"I was gonna go home," she shrugged. "Don't have to though."

"Come to my house," said Ziggy, her voice coming out dry. "We can say we're revising *Jane Eyre*."

Lena nodded, and they started walking up the street towards the church.

The sky was a stark, sunless shroud of grey. A low, creeping chill threaded through the breeze, enough to make Ziggy pull her sleeves down over her hands. Still, they didn't rush.

"It was fun the other night..." Lena said softly. "'Til it wasn't."

Ziggy nodded.

"Jamie said you had an argument yesterday... not that it's any of my business. I just don't think it's jealousy, if that's what you're worried about."

"What?" Ziggy asked flatly.

"I mean that's not why he's got a problem with Callum."

"I didn't think that," she heaved a sigh, a pain behind her eyes. "It's not that complicated."

"It kind of is," Lena shrugged. "I think he feels protective of you. Even now. But he knows it's not his place."

Ziggy wasn't sure that was it either, but she didn't think Lena would want to hear what she really thought. Who Callum reminded her of sometimes. Instead, she pulled a face.

"Ugh, boys. They need more protecting than we do."

"Exactly," huffed Lena. "Jamie's limping around like Tiny Tim, with some ancient Celtic hunter coming after him. And he thinks you can't handle Bart Simpson?"

Ziggy snorted. It turned into a proper laugh. Lena's frown dissolved into laughter too. They rounded the corner by the church just as the bell tolled one o'clock. Ziggy paused to peer in through the churchyard gates. A sudden breeze stirred the leaves in the churchyard, whispery and restless. Lena stopped next to her.

"Do you think something happened to him?" she asked softly.

"Yes," replied Ziggy. "I don't think he's coming back. He wanted to go."

"I wanted to go." Lena's eyes were on the rows of headstones too. "I thought I'd find Nicky. Or at least feel less like half a person and more like myself again... You think it'll be simple and safe down there, like being a little kid. But it's not like that."

Lena folded her arms across her chest as though warding off the cold. "It's dark," she said. "And quiet. You feel them start to chew at you from the inside. Not all at once. Just... little pieces of your soul, going missing."

"That's not what happened to Nicky..."

"No. He would have fought them," she smiled grimly.

Ziggy pictured Callum smoking his cigarette with grazed knuckles and inky fingers. The pink and blue beaded bracelet. *He wouldn't fight.* Her chest felt tight.

She said nothing. She reached out and picked up a brittle leaf caught in the church gate, crushing it between her fingers.

The church bell groaned once more, a minute late. They both flinched.

"Hey, come on..." Lena said softly. "Let's get going before it rains again." They turned away together.

* * *

The air inside the caravan was thick and still, like a jar sealed too long.

Without the wolf canvas propped in the corner, the space felt wrong. Ziggy kept glancing at the doorway. She half-expected to see something standing there.

She felt like she should have brought the painting back with her. Locked it behind a closed door. Bricked it up.

Lena inspected the hand-labeled bottles on the tabletop; lavender, foxglove, swirling the purplish contents.

"They'll turn brown over time," said Ziggy. "Once they're on a canvas, they won't stay purple."

Lena's brow furrowed.

"What's the point then?"

"Things change," Ziggy replied. "Nature." She lifted her shoulders. "Art."

"You drew the wall to keep Jamie safe," said Lena. "You drew that... thing with the horns when you didn't even know what it was. Could you draw it all just... going away?"

"I tried." Ziggy picked up her sketchbook and opened it to the page she had torn out at the tree stump. The page was loose and wrinkled but she hadn't thrown it away. "I don't know how to do it. Maybe I can make something but how do I unmake it?"

Lena took the loose sheet, turning it sideways.

"What's this supposed to be?"

"Nothing," Ziggy huffed. She cleared the table, shoving papers into a pile. A yellow Bic lighter slid out from under them. She pocketed it quickly, not wanting to look at it. "Angry scribbles. I don't know."

"Well… this is the stile on the flood bank, I can see that," Lena said. She tapped the jagged lines near the centre. "Look- the step, and the fence running either side."

Ziggy sat beside her, tilting her head. From this angle, it was unmistakable. Not just the stile, but the slope of the grass, the warped fence.

Lena pointed again, this time to the smudge just beneath the stile; a looping line with little dots scrawled around it.

"And what's *this*?"

Ziggy stared. The angry graphite marks had felt meaningless yesterday. Now they looked like something spilled. A frayed thread. Circles tumbling like dropped sweets.

"Beads," she whispered. "It's a broken bracelet."

***

After Lena went home, Ziggy went to her bedroom and tried to revise *Jane Eyre,* but her head swam with images of a bloody Converse trainer, a broken string of beads. A Swiss Army Knife stuck in a wooden fence.

The words in the book blurred in front of her eyes. She hadn't realised she was crying.

She picked up the musical shepherdess and wound up the wooden base, then placed it back down on her bedside table. The shepherdess turned slowly, her porcelain eyes blank. Ziggy curled up on her side and watched the figure revolve.

"Tell me what to do," she murmured.

The lilting, melancholy tune played on; familiar, aching, like someone calling a name in the dark.

She didn't expect an answer.

* * *

Ziggy ran. Breathing hard.

The wolf was close behind her. She felt its hot breath on her ankles; heard it growl as it snapped at the plastic Halloween cape that trailed behind her.

"Jamie!" her voice came out small. Weak.

He had escaped the churchyard this time. He ran ahead of her, scruffy trainers kicking up dust from the dirt path. A small boy, face painted white with black eyes. He looked back over his shoulder at her call, and she saw the whites of his eyes go wide behind his glasses.

"Ziggy! Run!"

The moon shone down on the hedgerows. An owl fled its perch in a tree, startled at their approach.

She risked a glance over her shoulder. Glimpsed black fur. Eyes. Teeth.

A hunting horn sounded somewhere in the distance.

Ziggy stumbled, foot catching on a branch, and fell. The dirt came up to meet her. Her face landed in the dust and her hand in a patch of flowers sprouting from the edge of the path.

Lavender.

This plant shouldn't be here, and neither should she.

She gripped a handful of it and pulled. The roots came up tangled in tiny white pearls.

Baby teeth.

She turned, rolling onto her back. She put a hand to the locket at her neck. And then the hulking black creature pounced. It snarled; a sound like thunder crashing underwater. Her bones rattled.

In a flash of yellow fangs, it snapped at her face. A metallic taste in her mouth. Her ears were ringing. The sound grew louder as she screamed.

* * *

Ziggy woke with her breath sharp in her throat. She choked on her tears, the taste of blood still lingering on her tongue. The shepherdess had stopped turning. Her phone was ringing on the bedside table.

She picked it up, slowly, wiping her face.

"Jamie…"

"Ziggy, listen… I shouldn't have said what I said," his voice was far away, but warm. "It wasn't about Callum, or you. It was about me… I'm scared."

Still trying to slow down the thump of her heart in her chest, Ziggy didn't say anything.

"You okay?" he asked.

"I can't do this on my own."

She didn't want to cry again. She wanted to believe someone meant it this time. That it wasn't just words. She heard him take a deep breath.

"Me neither… Can I come over; before it gets dark?"

Ziggy stared at her ceiling.

"Yeah. Bring your knife… And the poker."

Chapter 26

The summer they were twelve years old, Nicky and Lena's parents had taken them to the beach one day. They had an estate car with a pair of backwards facing seats in the boot, which they invited Jamie and Ziggy along to fill, entombed by towels and a striped windbreak. The coast was only two hours away, but Jamie spent the whole ride queasy from facing backward. Ziggy didn't like being able to see the stern eyes of lorry drivers frowning down from up high like angry predators of the road.

She turned around again to peer over the seat. Nicky was absorbed in his *Gameboy*, eyes fixed on the little screen in his hands, tongue poking out slightly between his teeth. She glanced at Jamie with a tiny smile, then reached over and tickled the back of Nicky's neck with a finger.

He slapped her hand.

"Ziggy! Shit! Wario, you bastard!"

Ziggy burst out laughing.

"Nicky!" his mother scolded from the front passenger seat. "One more, I mean it!"

"It's Justine! She's being an arsehole!" but he was laughing.

"Language! Nicky!" his mother gave an exasperated huff. "Can you please?" She turned to the twins' father.

"That's enough, Nick. Drop it."

Frank Meyer's low voice rumbled, but he was smiling in the rear-view mirror.

Nicky snorted. "I'll drop your Nan."

Ziggy caught his eye and grinned.

When they arrived at the beach, it was colder than they'd expected, despite the August sun, and she stayed wrapped in a slouchy Fair Isle cardigan that got caked with sand at the cuffs as she dug holes.

Lena, self-conscious with one of her brother's Adidas tee shirts over her swimming costume paddled near the edge of the water while the boys threw themselves at the waves like a pair of excited penguins. Jamie, shivering and constantly stepping on rocks that he couldn't see without his glasses, gave up sooner than Nicky, who didn't even need company to enjoy himself. He followed Ziggy up the rocks, towel around his shoulders, treading awkwardly on bare feet.

The sun had warmed her, and she took off her cardigan, spreading it on a large black rock to sit on, hugging her knees and watching Lena hop the breakers, spindly as Bambi on the ice, and Nicky bellowing that he had seen a jellyfish and sprinting for the shore.

"There's a cave up there," said Ziggy, indicating over her shoulder. "Shall we have a look?"

"Yeah, let me get my shoes."

"Catch me up."

She clambered over the stones towards the yawning mouth that opened up in the side of the black cliff face, glad that she had kept her flip-flops on. Back on the beach, Jamie was struggling to get sandy feet inside his trainers. He shouted to Lena, but she pulled a face and shook her head. Lately, she seemed to want to play with the boys less than she used to. People said that's growing up, but the idea of not being *the four of them* made Ziggy's tummy hurt.

Nicky was already hopping from rock to rock towards Ziggy, barefoot and heedless of the sharp edges of broken shells, scratchy dried seaweed and limpets clinging to the stones.

"How far does it go back?" he called.

Ziggy stopped at the entrance, which she knew was why he'd called out to her. He would've hated the thought of her getting there first. He stumbled and grazed his ankle on a rock, wincing, but then carried on as though nothing had happened.

"I can't tell, it's too dark," she said. "I think it's deep."

"Come on," he grinned at her, water still running from his hair. "You go first; you've got shoes on. But if there's a *Furby* with red eyes in there, we sacrifice Jamie."

Ziggy laughed, looking back down the beach for Jamie, who had only just got his shoes back on, but Nicky was already nudging her toward the cave mouth.

It was higher and wider than it had looked from down on the sand. A great black void in the side of the cliff, big enough to drive a car into. Ziggy pictured smugglers hauling crates through here centuries ago. The air smelled cold, briny and stale. Scattered charcoal from a recent fire peppered the sand.

"Watch your step," she told Nicky. "I bet there's plenty of toddler piss in here too."

Nicky followed her into the darkness. He picked up a tiny pebble and tossed it at the wall of the cave. The echo shimmered around them; a cold, hollow sound that seemed to bounce back for miles. Near the edges of the cave were rock pools, and Ziggy thought tiny creatures must be alive in there, but the dark swallowed everything.

CHAPTER 26

She'd expected silence, but the breeze whistled through the top of the cave and water dripped, steady as a pulse.

In the darkness, the cave was alive.

She felt Nicky's wet arm reach out for her and she turned her head to see the outline of his face as he let out a laugh that was all bravado.

"We could live here," he said, quiet enough that his voice didn't echo. "You and me."

Ziggy smiled cautiously. It wasn't always this easy with Nicky.

She peered deeper into the dark recesses of the cave.

"Are we going further in?"

He slipped past her, padding silently on the wet sand. Ziggy's own feet scuffed and flopped noisily, but Nicky disappeared like a ghost into the blackness.

She put her arms out blindly, feeling for the walls but stumbled a little over a small rock, regaining her footing clumsily. She heard him laugh again, from up ahead, the echo of his voice sounding alarmingly distant in the void.

How deep was it?

"Nick, I can't see you." She raised her voice, trying to keep it steady.

A reply echoed lightly off the walls, calling her name, but it wasn't Nicky. There was a lump in her throat now and she spun around, trying to see the light, trying to find her way back to the entrance.

"Ziggy!" Jamie's voice was far away.

She couldn't see him, but as she moved towards the sound, there was a crescent moon of light that showed her the way to go. She hadn't remembered turning a corner.

"Hold on, wait there!" she shouted back, hearing nerves

creep in at the edges of her voice. "It's really dark and I can't find Nicky."

The cave walls dripped around her. She felt something sharp poke into the bottom of her thin foam flip flop and crouched to pick out the quill of a matted grey seagull feather. In the dim half-light, she felt a tiny bit of the tension ease in her belly, knowing that Jamie was at the mouth of the cave.

But her eyes still searched the darkness for Nicky.

She called his name again. Only her own voice echoed in response. Ziggy squeezed her fists into tight balls at her sides.

"Oh my god, that's a massive crab!"

In a flurry of wet limbs, Nicky came barreling out of the dark. He crashed into her, catching hold of her arms, breathless with laughter.

"Wanna see it?" he asked. "It's not scary, I promise."

"Yeah, but-" she hesitated, trying to hold him still. "Don't disappear again. Wait for Jamie."

She could just about make out his grin, mischievous, but not unkind.

"Alright. Hold his hand." He looked back towards the light. "Come on Jim-Jam! I've found a girlfriend for you!"

Ziggy let out a relieved laugh. Nicky shook his head like a dog, splashing her with drips of salty water. He was still holding onto her forearms.

"How far does it go back?" she asked him.

He gave her a look that was at once teasing and deadly serious.

"Forever."

Chapter 27

"Do you know how many people in our year have got driving licenses already?"

Jamie was prodding a patch of brambles in the undergrowth with the iron poker while Ziggy stopped to tie her shoes. "I'm never getting out of this village."

"How many times has Luke failed his test though?"

He let out a small breath through his nose that might have been a laugh.

She stood up again and gave him a nudge. The sky was the same heavy grey as his eyes, and his hoodie was zipped up against the chill.

"It's gonna be okay," she said softly. "I've kind of got a plan."

"Kind of?"

She looked up the path, then said, "Yeah. I'm gonna bring the tree back." She had started walking again. Up ahead of them was the gravel path to where the stump of the old apple tree sat lonesome and squat in the late afternoon light.

Somewhere above them, a crow let out a low, laughing caw. Jamie said nothing, but he had stopped walking. She turned back around to face him.

"You look unimpressed," said Ziggy flatly.

"What does that even mean?" he asked. "You got apple seeds

in your pocket? Baby teeth?"

Her mouth twitched.

"Stupider than that."

Jamie's face hardened, and he looked away from her, pressing his lips together as though to keep something from slipping out.

"Jamie…" she said gently. "Come on. I'm not *trying* to be annoying. Let's keep walking, I'll tell you."

"Fine." He put up his hands. "It's only my life."

He scuffed through the dirt, dragging the poker along like he was trying to break the silence. The damp stump of the apple tree was sprouting rubbery grey mushrooms. Ancient as the hills, it had blossomed and borne fruit for generations, but now its corpse was rotting and soft. Ziggy wrinkled her nose at the sight of it.

"They're still out there…" she murmured.

"The- the children under the hill?"

She nodded.

"The tree's gone, but they're not."

"They must be… hungry."

Jamie swallowed a breath before he said it and his voice came out strangled. He looked like he wished he'd kept his mouth shut.

A dry gust rattled the hedge behind them. Ziggy glanced over her shoulder. Nothing there; just cow parsley and brambles, bent by the breeze. But her skin prickled like someone had just whispered her name.

They walked on past the stump and over the train tracks, the poker clanking across the metal like the toll of a bell as he dragged it. Some instinctive part of Ziggy wished he'd stop making so much noise and drawing attention to them. But he was already marked, they both knew that. There was nowhere he could go that he could escape them. They knew his blood, and it was theirs. He had left it for them on the apple tree four years ago.

"I've been drawing things that are real," said Ziggy. "And sometimes the things I draw *become* real..." she spoke slowly, choosing her words carefully. Jamie watched her, silently.

"You gave them your blood in exchange for Lena's soul- and I know you're gonna say you didn't-" she smiled a little. "It was nowhere near that dramatic. I was there. You didn't know what you were doing... That's how they trick you."

Jamie kicked a stone along the path. He nodded.

"The tree was a seal. I'm just gonna paint a new one." She shrugged. He frowned.

"That's really stupid."

"I *told* you it was stupid. Have you got a better plan? The blood moon's tomorrow."

He looked out over the fields as he walked, chewing the inside of his cheek.

"You're probably the best chance I've got," he murmured.

Ziggy didn't quite know what to say to that. She gripped the sleeves of her hoodie tightly in her fists.

The sky was heavy and grey overhead, threatening rain again, but it was still hours until sunset; until the beast would be lurking. The poker scraped along the dirt.

At the edge of her vision, something moved. Black, fast, crawling the inside of the hedge. She whipped her head toward it.

Nothing.

"Did you see that?"

Jamie frowned. "What?"

"Never mind."

"You never used to get scared," he said quietly.

"The real world always scared me more than monsters… I think that's why I drew them, y'know? It wasn't that I didn't care about Nicky or Lena. Drawing them made me feel stronger. I could never draw how I really felt…"

Jamie looked at his shoes as he walked and nodded slowly, brows drawn together thoughtfully, but he didn't answer. The wind moved through the hedgerow, making her shiver.

"Look-"

A pointed black shape stuck out of the hedge. Callum's bike. Ziggy's heart jumped to her throat, and she jogged towards it.

The bike lay on its side, front wheel in the air. This was where most of the damage was; the tyre was half knocked off the rim. The handlebar, buried in leaves, was bent at a crooked angle that made the whole thing look drunk. It looked like it shouldn't have made it a hundred yards, let alone the three miles from town where the accident had happened.

Ziggy stomach turned.

"I can't believe he got back on that thing…" said Jamie, obviously thinking the same. "What the hell was in his head?"

"He's not like us," said Ziggy.

"Smart?"

"Lucky."

The flood bank was up ahead. Jamie walked on, leaving Ziggy staring at the rusty frame in the hedge, her stomach in knots.

The path slanted up and there was a section of new fence where the old stile used to be. It was no longer a public footpath. The cows grazing on the slope had gone still. Their heads turned in quiet unison, black eyes placid. One blinked its long eyelashes at them but didn't move.

Jamie looked out over the flood bank, towards the stream in the distance. Lena's name wasn't carved into the wood there anymore.

He swore under his breath and pointed.

Ziggy's heart thumped, and she followed his finger with her eyes.

There was a shape in the grass on the slope. Not moving. For a split second, Ziggy wasn't sure it was him. His knees were bent up to the sky, just like the other day in the park but his arms were splayed awkwardly like a dropped marionette.

Ziggy remembered lying in that spot herself, some fifty metres from the fence, plenty of times, with Jamie at her side, one earphone each, staring at the sky. She couldn't tell if his eyes were open though.

"Is he alive?" Jamie put a hand on the fence. "Callum!"

The body in the grass didn't move and Jamie started to climb. Ziggy caught his sleeve.

"Wait," she said. "This is too easy. What if he's like Lena was?"

"What if he's not? Besides," he half-lifted the poker. "We've got iron."

Ziggy's breath hitched, and she looked around.

"Is there a bull?" she asked.

"I don't know. Wait there."

Jamie climbed over the fence. She saw him wince as he jumped down onto his bad leg. Brow furrowed, she climbed over after him.

The cows began to amble lazily away, calling to each other in deep, throaty voices. The one closest to Callum's prone body seemed to notice him for the first time and swerved to avoid stepping on him as it passed. Callum didn't flinch.

They approached him together, Ziggy calling his name again. He stirred as she dropped to her knees at his side, cautiously taking in his battered form.

"Callum, wake up," she said gently.

He rubbed his eyes and grumbled, frowning, like she was telling him he was late for school.

He still had the bracelet on his wrist. It wasn't broken at all.

Maybe it wasn't too late.

Ziggy's fingers grazed the hair at his temple, where it was dark with blood. It was dry and crusty. He didn't react to her touch. His face was bone grey, and his lips were cracked.

Jamie gave him a shove. Not gentle.

"Hey. Sit up."

Slowly, as though he'd forgotten how to move, Callum pushed himself upwards. The sleeve of his hoodie was ripped and there was blood on his arm too. His knees hadn't fared much better.

"The police have been looking for you," said Jamie with urgency. "Everyone's been worried."

Callum blinked a few times, then finally his pale eyes registered Ziggy and the ghost of a smile flickered across his face.

"Are you okay?" her voice came out tight.

He didn't answer. He put his hand out to touch hers; his fingers trembling. His palm was raw and studded with grit. Ziggy turned it over carefully in her own.

"Mate, you know you got hit by a car yesterday, yeah? Do you remember?" Jamie said. "You've hit your head. You can't just sit in a field."

"Is it..." Callum let out a shaky breath. "Is it Monday?"

Ziggy flinched. The way he said it, like 'Monday' was a word from another language.

"Yeah," she nodded.

"Come on, get up." Jamie stooped to grip Callum at the elbow and haul him to his feet. With surprising surety, he put both hands on the shorter boy's shoulders and looked him straight in the eyes. "Do you feel sick?"

Callum shook his head slowly. Ziggy remembered Jamie's first aid training and realised he was trying to ascertain if he was concussed or just stoned.

Or maybe something else.

"You alright?" Jamie asked, frowning.

"It's not so bad," Callum lifted his shoulders. "I don't feel anything now."

Chapter 28

Callum pushed his bike; cigarette balanced between his lips. He caught Ziggy's eye and smiled like they shared a secret.

"Don't do that, I'm annoyed at you," she said.

"Why?"

"Because I thought you were dead or something. I texted you. Loads."

She frowned at the dirt and stomped on a twig. A few paces behind, Jamie swung the poker at the hedge, making enough noise to prove he wasn't eavesdropping.

Callum chewed his lip and said nothing. He looked genuinely flummoxed, as though the idea of someone caring about whether he answered was a puzzle he hadn't solved yet.

Eventually, he flicked the smoking end of his cigarette into the hedge. The moment it left his fingers, he seemed to shrink into himself. His inky thumb started drumming on the handlebar. A hollow, rhythmic sound. Ziggy couldn't stop watching it, but it made her insides twist uncomfortably.

"Sorry," he murmured. "I wasn't... I didn't think..."

"It's okay." She put her hand on top of his to stop it moving. His skin felt cold. "I'll let you off. You were having a bad day... A quick *'I'm alive'* would've been nice though."

"Noted."

They walked on. Overhead, the sky bruised darker, and the wind shifted, sharp with the smell of distant rain. Callum should have been soaked, or limping, or… something. But he wasn't.

"They arrested your stepdad," said Jamie, voice flat behind them.

Callum scoffed. "Hope he doesn't drop the soap."

Ziggy winced. She didn't have a response for that. They walked on and she kept her hand over Callum's, until he stopped dead, the motion so abrupt she stumbled. He turned sharply, peering behind them.

Jamie froze mid-swing, eyes suddenly alert. He gripped the poker like a bat.

"What?" Ziggy asked. Her pulse ticked up.

Callum stared past Jamie's shoulder, eyes wide, locked on something none of them could see.

"Do I have to…" he whispered. His voice sounded younger. Like a child hiding something under his bed and hoping it wouldn't bite.

Ziggy looked at Jamie. He met her eyes, tight-lipped, and gave a small nod.

"Yes," she said. She grabbed Callum's arm and turned him. "We're going back before it gets dark. You need to talk to the police and wash your face."

"I'm not- I can't- "

Panic twisted his features. His fingers slipped on the handlebars like he was about to bolt. His eyes moved; fast, jerky, like a wasp caught on a window. It made Ziggy's chest tighten with unease.

He almost dropped the bike, then gripped it harder, knuckles pale.

"I don't want to talk to the police," he said. "Or my mum. I can't go home. It's my fault. All of it."

Ziggy didn't let go of his sleeve.

"Fine. Don't go home. Come to mine. Hide in the caravan if you want."

She tugged at his arm.

"But we *can't* stay out here."

The wind picked up again, stronger this time. Jamie was at their side now, stumbling a little on his injured leg.

"Come on, mate. You're good at art too, right? You can help us. Ziggy, tell him about your plan. It's stupid, he'll love it."

***

Ziggy let out a frustrated groan. She leaned over the table, took the rubber Jamie had been fidgeting with from his hand and began scrubbing at the paper again.

Callum sat next to her. He'd found a pair of scissors and was cutting random shapes in a piece of paper he'd picked up from the floor.

"Were you thinking about me when you did this?" he asked, turning over the sheet with the sharp angular charcoal lines of a brick wall drawn on it.

"I was thinking about a strange, disturbing creature," she replied wryly. "So, pretty close."

He'd become more animated since she'd brought him a sandwich from the house. He'd washed in the sink while she was gone. When she'd come back, sandwich and *Twix* in hand, Jamie, grim-faced, stuck a dressing on his elbow and raised an eyebrow at Ziggy.

"You don't want to see this man shirtless," he said. "Looks like a Picasso painting. Very sad."

Callum's mouth twitched at that. He blinked hesitantly at the sandwich but then thanked her and wolfed it down in a few bites. Then, suddenly energised, he jumped up to make tea for them all. Ziggy looked over at him, distracted from her drawing by his clattering in the cupboards.

"Got any coffee?"

Ziggy shook her head, sharpening a pencil.

"Tea'll do," he said too quickly.

He spooned sugar into his like it would fix everything and then climbed back into the corner seat between Ziggy and the wall to play with scissors.

Jamie sat quietly and watched her draw. She looked at the old drawing of the tree that was stuck to the wall behind his head and tried to recreate the lines on the paper in front of her. Her stomach knotted. They were too widely spaced; it didn't look like the same tree. Jamie glanced over his shoulder at it, then back at the picture on the table, his face unreadable, but calm.

Ziggy kept her eyes on the page. If she looked at Jamie, she might start crying. If she looked at Callum, she might scream.

She sighed heavily. "I can't do this. It's not coming out right."

Her pencil snapped again.

Frustrated, she growled and threw it down on the table. It bounced and landed in Jamie's lap. He picked it up silently and started sharpening it.

"You're thinking too much," said Callum. He opened the *Twix* and dipped it in his tea.

All the muscles in Ziggy's neck were tense. She frowned at him.

"You're not as helpful as you think."

Callum squinted at the drawing. He leaned over, sliding some of the jagged strips of cut-up paper across the page, over the top of the lines she'd drawn. He lined the shapes up haphazardly. Then added a couple and adjusted them so that they formed the shape of a crooked tree trunk.

"Mixed media," he murmured, licking chocolate off his mouth.

Ziggy pressed her lips together, moved a piece of paper slightly, so that it looked more like a branch.

"Yeah, that's better," she said. "Jamie, pass me those brushes; in the jar behind you." Ziggy collected the bottles of homemade ink from the shelf above her head and handed a small glue stick to Callum. "Here, keep going."

"Cutting and sticking. Much more my speed," he said with a smile that didn't quite reach his eyes.

Jamie turned his head and peered out the window. The sky was starting to darken.

"How long do you reckon you've been doing this?" he asked, looking back at the new lines Ziggy was brushing; sweeping strokes of dark purple foxglove ink outlining the cut-up bits of brick wall sketch that Callum was gluing into place.

"Doing what?" she brushed her hair from her face.

Jamie was watching her hand move with the fascination of a child watching a magician, trying to spot the trick.

"When we were little, you used to draw scary things that turned out to be real," he said. "But did you draw them because you knew they were real, or did they become real because you drew them?"

She shook her head.

"They've been here longer than us. I drew the stories Nana

Peg told me."

"It's since they took one of your drawings," said Callum lightly. "They really like your work."

"What?" Ziggy's hand froze, and she turned to him. He carried on snipping paper, without looking at her.

"You know, a few years ago or whenever. Didn't one of them take something you'd drawn? It had your name at the bottom too," he smiled at her like it was a joke. "Not your *real* name though."

"How the hell do you know about that?"

Callum hesitated, shifted in his seat.

"I had this insane nightmare a while ago- I thought I told you about it." Now he looked at her, blinking slowly. "It was about that wolf in the churchyard- chasing a little kid in a skeleton costume." He glanced at Jamie. "But then it chased me instead. I got away on my bike... Did I seriously not tell you this?" he smiled, but he looked anxious.

"Go on," Ziggy prompted, fingers twitching. She knew what was coming. She'd been there too, in the dream. But she needed to hear it out loud.

"I rode out to the train tracks and under the apple tree there were all these pages, like they'd been torn from a sketchbook." Callum's hand moved towards hers on the table, but he didn't touch her. "And one of them was signed *Justine Briggs*."

Ziggy finally exhaled. She remembered the sketch of the tree, signed with her name, crumpled in the creature's hand that day four years ago. And in her dream. Jamie had gone pale and gripped a paintbrush so tightly in his fist that it snapped. She didn't need him to say that he'd had the same dream too. He looked out of the window again at the tall yew trees, silhouetted against the murky sky.

"I need to go home," he said tightly. "I don't want to be outside when it gets properly dark."

"Yeah," Ziggy nodded stiffly. "Take that with you," she pointed to the poker leaning against the cupboard door. "I'll keep doing this."

Jamie got up and opened the door. A sharp breeze lifted the edge of the paper and Callum caught a few pieces that threatened to fly off the table. Jamie beckoned Ziggy with his head, and she stood up to follow him outside.

"Jamie!" Callum called before the door closed. Jamie looked back inside, Callum spoke without looking at him. "Thanks."

Alone in the garden, in the dim evening light, the wind whipping leaves around them, Ziggy looked down at Jamie's trainers, grubby from the afternoon's walk.

"You don't have to tell me there's something wrong with him, I've got eyes."

"I wasn't gonna say that…" he said. His fingers twitched at his side. "I just… want to make sure you're okay."

Ziggy nodded. She wasn't okay. And he wasn't either. She pulled him into a hug, wrapping her arms tightly around his middle.

She'd kissed him once when they were fourteen, play-acting at being the hero in a story, and she'd held his hand when they were scared. But she couldn't remember the last time she had hugged her best friend. He was much taller than her now. He squeezed her shoulders and didn't quite manage to stifle a sniff.

"I don't know if it'll be okay," she said.

Chapter 29

Ziggy paused in the doorway, toast cooling on the plate in her hand. The cold grey light from outside landed on the picture she and Callum had completed last night. Setting the plate of toast down on the table next to it, she reached over to open the curtain so that she could see it properly.

It was a beautiful image, in a strange, otherworldly way. A mess of scribbled pencil lines, jagged scraps of charcoal scratched paper, shadows soaked with ink. The colours were all wrong; foxglove purple bark for the tree trunk, pale lavender leaves, apples pale and pearly like lost teeth hanging from the branches.

This wasn't the tree she remembered; this was a tree made of her own soul. But it wasn't alive yet.

Callum was still asleep on the bench seat by the table, half covered in a blanket, one foot on the floor, like he was prepared to run out the door at any moment.

"I brought you some toast," she said quietly. He blinked and sat up slowly, rubbing his eyes. She was about to sit down opposite him when he shifted over. "You okay?"

He nodded, but squinted into the light, eyes flicking to the window. He touched the side of his head gingerly. When Ziggy sat down beside him, he leaned into her the same way Puck did. She half expected him to chirrup.

"Didn't sleep much. I had a bad dream," she said.

He turned his head to her questioningly. His eyes looked as heavy as hers felt.

"I dreamed that my feet turned into roots," she continued. "My skin was bark, and every tiny gust of wind made my arms shake."

Callum didn't answer. He took her hand, turned it over in his as though checking it really was made of skin, and then laced his fingers with hers. Ziggy's throat felt tight.

"I couldn't move," her voice came out thin. Her eyes prickled with tears. "I couldn't scream. I just had to watch as the wolf ripped him apart, and you…"

"What?"

"You were eating a *Twix*."

Callum snorted. Ziggy laughed and wiped away a tear as it spilled over her eyelashes.

"Jesus…" he picked up a slice of toast and took a bite. "Let me know when I do something heroic or sexy in your dreams, yeah?"

"That's the only place it's likely to happen."

He laughed softly and tilted his head against her shoulder a little, eyes half closed.

"It's not finished, is it?" he asked, gesturing to the picture on the table with his toast.

Ziggy shook her head.

"Something's missing. We don't have time. It's tonight." She gave his hand a little squeeze. "You seem better," she said, not sure if she meant it. "You should call your mum… Or someone. Your brother and sister must be really worried."

He put the toast down and stared at the table.

"I know," he said eventually. "I will. Not yet."

* * *

Lena stood among the cardboard boxes in the Briggs' kitchen, arms folded, eyeing Callum warily through the window as he stood out in the garden smoking.

"Are we just pretending he hasn't been wearing the same clothes for three days?"

"Yes," Ziggy said flatly. "Same way we're pretending I can stop Jamie getting dragged to hell with a tree drawing."

Lena smiled gently. She looked back at the picture unfurled on the kitchen table. It looked out of place here among the salt and pepper shakers and china fruit bowl. A weird blip. A Venus Flytrap in a rose garden.

"It's a good tree though. I like the colours. It looks... dreamy."

"That's good?"

"Well, it's not a nightmare."

Jamie arrived, grey faced and rumpled. Ziggy put the kettle on, like it was just another Tuesday.

"Is this what it's like to be an adult?" wondered Jamie, watching the milk swirl in his cup. "Making tea and worrying about death?"

"I think so," said Ziggy. "Also hoovering."

Lena was the first to laugh, letting out an undignified snort. Ziggy giggled, holding her stomach, and Jamie coughed into his tea.

Lena was still laughing against Jamie's shoulder when Callum came inside. He hovered by the door, his hand held out to the cat, but Puck bolted outside the moment it opened. He looked vaguely disappointed at the feline snub, but sat down at the table next to Ziggy, where there was a cup of coffee waiting for him. His shoulders hunched like he was cold.

"What's so funny?" he asked.

"Honestly- nothing," said Jamie. "Ever. Not my life. Not this." He gestured to the picture on the table. "I don't even *know* what that is."

Callum shrugged, frowning.

"Art, innit."

"Will you lot stop?" Lena hiccoughed; but she wasn't smiling now.

Leaning against the kitchen counter, Jamie put an arm around her and squeezed her shoulder. A heaviness had settled in Ziggy's stomach.

"It's not done yet," she nodded at the picture then turned to look at Callum.

He had picked up a sharpie pen from the top of a box of books on the floor and was doodling on the leg of his jeans. He'd drawn fangs and beady eyes around the hole at his knee so that the torn fabric looked like a monster's gaping mouth.

"You haven't signed it," he murmured. "That's what's missing. Your name." He held out the pen to her. "It's *your* artwork, isn't it?"

"My name…" Ziggy stared at him but didn't take it. He held her gaze steady, like a dare. The skin on the back of her neck prickled.

"Are you trying to trick me?"

He was fighting a smile. Failed. Looked away before she did. "If I am, I'm a bit shit at it."

Ziggy took the pen from him.

She reached towards the picture. Jamie stood up straight

abruptly, dropping his arm from Lena's shoulder.

"I think he's right," said Ziggy. She looked between Jamie and Lena; both of them now watching her with matching expressions of alarm. Callum was looking at the floor, chewing his lip and tapping his thumb against his knee without rhythm.

Jamie came towards her as though he was going to take the pen from her hand.

"Ziggy, wait-"

But before he could stop her, she scribbled her name. Not Justine Briggs, her *true* name, *Ziggy*, on the trunk of the tree. Carved into the paper like the names of lost children had been carved into the bark in years gone by.

The moment her pen left the paper, the room felt still. Like the tree was listening.

"You didn't havc to do that. You know what happens if they get your name. It's like an invitation." Jamie's voice was a harsh whisper. He turned an accusing glare on Callum. *"She didn't have to do that."*

Ziggy's heart fluttered in her chest, but she felt oddly calm. She handed the pen back to Callum, stilling his fingers.

"No, but I did it anyway," she said, surprised at how even her voice came out. "It's my name and my tree. *Not theirs.* It wasn't finished."

"Is it finished now?" asked Lena.

Ziggy looked at the picture. Her tree.

Our tree.

She turned back to Callum, nodded at the pen in his hand.

He smiled; with something like relief, leaned over and wrote his name on one of the branches. He scrawled it so fast he missed an L, swore under his breath, then went back to add it. He held the pen out to Jamie with an infuriating twitch of his lips.

"Don't s'pose you fancy doing it in blood?"

Jamie took the pen. He turned to Ziggy.

"I just want it on record that I'm against this," he said. "But I trust you."

He wrote his name on the trunk of the tree, below Ziggy's. His hand was shaking.

Lena looked furious as she snatched the pen from him.

"I agree with Jamie."

She yanked the paper across the table and wrote her own name in angry block capitals on one of the branches then turned her icy gaze on Callum.

"My brother would have agreed with you," she said.

Next to her name she wrote *Nicky*. The childish scrawl, the looping Y. She shoved the pen into Callum's chest. "Now will you please go home and shower?"

Chapter 30

Ziggy watched Callum hop down from sitting on the wall outside the house. The car had barely stopped. The driver left the door swinging open and the engine running as she jumped out. Ziggy could hear her swear at him, even through the closed front window, but his mother had tears on her cheeks. She took his face in both her hands and spoke so emphatically that his shoulders dropped even lower.

She wrapped her arms around him, his head sinking to her shoulder. His arms stayed by his sides. He wasn't much taller than her, a thin woman with bleached hair showing dark roots. Her eyes, too far apart just like his, rose up to the sky briefly as she hugged him. Ziggy felt like she shouldn't be watching, but she had to know he was okay.

Callum must have said something then, because she laughed, a watery, pained smile, and Ziggy could tell she was swearing at him again. She gave him a little shake, then nodded to the car. They were gone with a squeal of tyres, as quickly as the car had appeared.

"He- he'll come back for his bike," Ziggy said quietly, turning around to her mother, but not quite meeting her eye. "It needs fixing."

June's eyebrows twitched upwards.

"Needs scrapping." Her arms were folded, and her gaze was steady. "How long were you hiding him down there?"

"Only since yesterday afternoon. I'm sorry Mum, it wasn't-"

"You're not a child, Justine," said June. The hardness in her voice gave Ziggy a jolt, and she turned her head back towards the window. "I understand there are things you won't always tell me. But if you'd trust me just once..."

June's fingers tapped against her elbow. Silence hung in the air, heavy as iron.

Ziggy pulled her sleeves down over her hands.

"I've got revision to do," she murmured, and slipped past her mother to the stairs.

* * *

Inky black, spiderwebbing through the pencil-shaded soil like fingers. Ziggy knew she wasn't imagining it. She hadn't drawn them and neither had Callum.

The tree on the page was alive and it was taking root.

In the quiet of her bedroom, she could hear the rustle of the breeze through its pale purple leaves. She didn't know if it was enough to stop what was coming for Jamie, but she knew it was something, and it didn't belong to the creatures that lived under the flood banks or any God of the Underworld. It belonged to her. She had done it.

Her fingers went instinctively to the locket at her neck.

I know you have a hard time remembering that sometimes.

She rubbed her eyes and stared at her English Literature notes, not reading, just listening to the whisper of the branches. The gentle shifting of earth as the roots settled deeper.

The soft thud of a falling apple.

She closed her eyes. Outside her window, the wind was picking up.

* * *

Evening settled over the house like dust, soft and quiet. Ziggy had fallen asleep by accident, head on her English notes, the cold edge of the desk pressed into her cheek.

In the dream she heard hooves. They struck the ground not like horses but like hollow drums.

The apple tree was the one from her picture. All purple, like heart's blood. Full of eyes instead of leaves. In the roots: teeth. In the branches: a voice calling her name, over and over, but each time it sounded more like a hunter's horn.

She jerked awake to darkness, heart pounding. Her phone buzzed: three texts from Callum.

19.53pm: **its coming**

20.10pm: **I no what 2 do**

20.13pm: **dont let jamie go out**

She brushed the hair from her face, a throb blooming behind her eyes, and phoned him. His voice was buffeted by the wind when he answered.

"-not ignoring you this time."

"Congratulations. What are you doing, where are you?"

"Don't worry. I'm fine- always am. Just… don't go out."

She could picture his smile. Endearing, deflecting. It made her eye twitch.

"Fuck that. No." She sat up straight, "Callum, I'm serious, tell me what's going on. I had a dream-"

"Me too-"

"I'm scared." Tears sprang to her eyes as the words fell out of her mouth.

"I'm not."

"*You're* scaring me. I need you to tell me the truth."

The sound of the wind whipped at the phone again. For a moment she thought he wasn't going to respond.

"It's going to take something," he said. "A soul. We can't stop it. You can't stop it." There was a long pause while she heard him fumble with the phone. "It doesn't have to be him."

Ziggy meant to sound fierce, to tell him off, but her voice came out small and cracked.

"What do you mean?"

"I'm sorry," he said. "I know I still owe you seven."

The phone went dead. Ziggy stared at it in her hand for a moment, eyes blurred by tears, chest thumping.

Then the doorbell rang. Once, twice. A sharp, panicked sound.

"Jamie…" she almost knocked over her chair getting up, but by the time she got downstairs, her mother was already opening the front door.

Lena was zipped into a green parka. Her windswept hair stuck to her cheeks as she pushed it out of her eyes, blinking past June, straight at Ziggy.

"He's gone."

Lena was breathless, wild-eyed. Ziggy stared at her, mouth dry. "It's coming for him. I heard it."

Ziggy nodded mutely, her mind already racing.

It's going to take something.

"What's going on?" June looked between them, frowning.

"I've just come from Jamie's house, he's not there." Lena's voice was desperate and shaky. She stepped inside and reached for Ziggy's hand. From the sleeve of her coat, Nicky's watch glinted in the light. "His sister said he was acting weird. Quiet. Just walked out the door and didn't say anything."

"Justine?" her mother spoke softly.

Ziggy's hand went to her locket.

It doesn't have to be him.

She turned to June then, wishing she stood taller. Wishing her voice sounded braver.

"I'm sorry Mum, it's hard to explain."

The sadness in her mother's eyes hurt her more than anger, or even disappointment would have. She searched for the right words. "Jamie's in trouble. I think I'm the only one who can help."

June closed her eyes and sighed.

"Alright," she said. "Can I do anything?"

Ziggy hesitated, knowing it sounded ridiculous.

"Can you find me a shovel? I need to plant a tree."

Chapter 31

The moon was swollen and red as a wound. It hung low over the rooftops, brighter than Ziggy could ever remember seeing it, giving the air an odd tinge. Like being underwater when blood had been spilled.

She thought of Nicky's shoe floating in the stream again and bit back nausea.

The wind had a strange, bone-deep chill. She tightened her coat around her, squeezing her fist around the handle of the weed fork. Not a shovel, but it would do.

She couldn't remember if it was the same weed fork she had used to plant the lavender with Nana Peg, or even the same one she had carried in her backpack to ward off an attack from a creature wearing Lena's face four years ago. That one, she was sure, had been lost on the flood bank, but there was something comforting about carrying an object that had served her well once before.

She hoped that Jamie had his Swiss Army Knife in his pocket too.

Beside her, Lena walked fast, boots crunching against gravel, the painting rolled up in her hand. The path turned to mud, and they left behind the last amber glow of streetlight.

The wind whistled through the hedgerows like a warning.

Somewhere out in the fields, something howled. At least it *sounded* like a howl. It could have been a fox. It could have been the wind. It could have been-

"The hunter's horn," Lena whispered.

Ziggy nodded. The sound drew her feet forward, tugging downward with each step, like she was rooted to the path. She glanced at Lena and saw her look over her shoulder, as though she might be having second thoughts. But she too moved as if compelled by the sound of the horn.

Perhaps she was. They had all known the call of the children under the hill.

Above them, the moon stared down unblinking.

Ziggy's heart beat in her throat. She could feel the boundary thinning with each step; between dream and waking, between myth and memory. Like falling asleep on her feet.

She didn't say anything, just picked up her pace, trainers squelching in the mossy earth. A few paces ahead, the tree stump came into view, damp and decaying, sprouting mushrooms like parasites.

Just as she knew he would be, Callum was standing next to it.

Hands in pockets. Waiting.

He threw up his hands in exasperation when he saw them.

"I told you not to come," he said.

"And *I told you* not to do anything stupid like getting killed," she spat back.

"I know what I'm doing."

He put a hand out to touch hers but she snatched it out of his grasp. He blinked, surprised.

Lena rolled her eyes.

"This from a man who can't even spell his own name. Have

you seen Jamie?"

He shook his head, still looking at Ziggy like he was worried she might turn him to stone. The wind whipped her hair. A distant mechanical rumble stilled the air, barely audible at first. She thought she heard the hunter's horn again but this time it was the high whistle of a train approaching.

Ziggy's hands went automatically to her ears as the train roared past, metal clanging on metal, the whistle screaming. The glow from the windows lit up their faces in flashes.

She took a step closer to Callum, as though he could shield her from the noise, even though she was angry with him, and Lena put a hand on her arm.

The noise died down, but it still rang unpleasantly in her ears.

Lena lifted her head sharply. "Did you hear that?"

Ziggy froze. At first, she thought it was just the wind again, but then she heard it too. A thud, then scrambling footsteps. From the direction of the fields.

"Jamie?" she called.

No answer. But then; a shout. Panicked. Her name.

She squinted into the darkness beyond the train tracks, the hedges and fields lay murky in moonlight, jagged shadows of trees cutting shadows across the undergrowth.

"Ziggy!"

The wind carried his voice to her.

"Over there," she said on a breath, and took off without waiting for a response. Lena was right behind her, paint-stained paper clutched to her chest. Callum swore and followed. She bolted across the train tracks, ignoring the familiar muddy lane. Tonight, it was no safer than the road to hell.

Instead, she plunged into the hedge, aiming in the direction she had heard Jamie's voice. The undergrowth clawed at her legs as she tore through it, feebly pushing back branches with her weed fork. In all the times they had been across the tracks, they had never ventured into the fields before.

Ziggy tripped, Callum caught her arm and pulled a branch aside so that she and Lena could get past, out of the grappling branches and into the edge of the field. Lena's head whipped around like a rabbit out in the open.

The stump was a vague smudge behind them now. Ahead, the crops swayed under the red eye of the moon, shifting like a tide in the wind.

"Ziggy!"

She nearly sobbed when she saw him. He stumbled toward them, mud on his hands, blood on his forehead from a thin scratch. His jacket was torn, one sleeve gaping. Eyes like an animal in a trap.

"Which way-" he gasped, skidding to a stop when he saw Callum, fumbling over his words. "I- You... The hunter called me out here, but now we're all in danger. *You* made us put our names on that tree- like it was a game."

Callum held up both hands, breathless, shaking his head. "No. I'm trying to stop it. It doesn't have to be you."

"It doesn't have to be *anyone*," Ziggy snapped.

She moved to Jamie, touched his hand. He was cold, clammy. Alive. "It didn't get you."

"It nearly did."

"Where is it now?" Lena asked, her voice thin.

Jamie turned and looked behind him. The field was quiet. Still. But for a moment, a flicker of black moved through the crops in the distance. There, then gone.

"It's close," Jamie said. "We don't have long. What's the plan?"

Ziggy reached for the locket around her neck. She turned to face Callum. "You said it doesn't have to be him. How do you know that?"

He looked away too quickly.

"The tree-" his eyes darted to the paper in Lena's hands. She held it like it was made of something poisonous. "It's a seal, just like you wanted. It doesn't have anybody's blood on it."

Jamie's hands curled into fists at his sides. "But it has *all* our names. I don't want to lose any more friends because he was feeling impulsive."

Lena put her hand on his arm, eyes darting about, watchful. Callum shrank back.

"I can hear it," he said, voice shaky. "Everything's always-*always* too loud but this is..." he trailed off hopelessly, covered his face with both hands.

Ziggy moved closer to him.

"This seal belongs to me. It's not theirs to twist into a price; I made it. I'm not letting them take *anybody*." She lowered her voice. "Not even you. Did you already forget that I said I quite like you?"

He dropped his hands and looked at her, doubtful.

"You said you like me a *bit*."

Ziggy's chest ached. She wanted to cry, or scream, or kiss him. Instead, she gave him a shove. "Come on."

Chapter 32

Her dreams had always started in the churchyard. It was, after all, right outside her window. But they'd always been leading here. Back to where it all began.

Ziggy gripped Callum's hand, but it was Lena she followed blindly through the crops. The stalks closed in around them as they ran, the sodden earth sucking at their feet with every step. Behind them, branches snapped and crunched.

Ziggy didn't dare look back. The sound was unmistakable. Heavy footfalls, snarling breath. Hooves sinking into wet earth.

The wolf was not alone.

The horn blew again, summoning a gust of wind, and the smell of iron and rot. Without the dirt track to follow, Ziggy couldn't tell which way to go. The field seemed endless, and the crops disguised hidden dips and ridges in the earth, but Lena ran ahead; her eyes locked on some unseen thread only she could follow.

"This way!" she gasped, already veering toward the flood bank.

Jamie stumbled after her. When he looked back at Ziggy, the moonlight hollowed his eyes, his face all bone and shadow.

Ziggy looked down at herself, half expecting to see that ridiculous Halloween dress. But she wasn't dreaming, and the hand that pulled Callum along in the dark wasn't wearing plastic witch fingers either.

Even the barbed wire fence didn't slow Lena down when she reached it. She found a section that was slung low, and lifted a leg over, barely pausing, as though she *knew* where she was going.

Jamie followed, awkwardly lifting his injured leg over. Ziggy hesitated.

"Where are the cows?" she asked. They were here yesterday, but the herd was nowhere in sight.

In the dark, she couldn't even hear their lowing. They had moved off silently, somewhere away from this corner, perhaps sensing what was coming.

Callum bumped into her as he clambered over the fence, looking anxiously over his shoulder.

"Why're we stopping?"

Lena froze. She was pale faced and staring at the flood bank. The place she hadn't returned to in four years. Her voice came out in a whisper. "Nick…" Ziggy went to her. "He's with us," Lena breathed, touching her fingers, eyes reflecting the moon. She pointed up ahead.

Ziggy nodded. Of course. Nicky always had a plan.

She started up the slope of the flood bank, leading the way. In the daylight at the top, you could see for miles, the achingly long, curving spine of grass. But in the dark it was just sky and stars. The watery red moon floating in the vast blackness.

They'd been nine years old the first time they came here, sweaty and sunburned, chasing Nicky to get him to share his *Chewits*. They'd barrel rolled down the slope until they were green, threw stones in the stream, and tried, unsuccessfully, to climb a tree for spiky conker shells. They watched trains go past and shouted at them.

Here in the dark, they were children again. Frightened, but together. Frantically, stupidly, together.

Ziggy dropped to her knees and began to dig. The weed fork stuck awkwardly in the grass; not the ideal tool, but it prized up a stone to get her started.

Callum joined in, clawing at the dirt with his fingers like he'd been waiting for this moment for years. Jamie pulled wet soil aside, and Lena, her breath catching, turned her head to the edge of the field.

"Ziggy…" she whispered.

"I know."

A shadow loomed there. Hulking, black and rotten. *What was it waiting for?*

The wolf needed only to strike, and it could rip them all to shreds. The horn called again, closer. Ever closer. The wolf was waiting for its master.

The hole was deep enough for her wrist, cold and damp. But the earth was alive.

Worms and beetles and next year's daisies. Food for the birds and all the other creatures that lived here. Ziggy held her hand out to Lena for the painting.

She unrolled it on the ground. The purple tree had grown so many more shiny white apples since this morning. And more names were carved into its bark: *Luke, Felicity, Peter…* She couldn't make them all out in the dark.

"Burying this will make it stop?" Jamie asked. His eyes were sharply focused on the picture, as though he couldn't bring himself to look back over his shoulder.

"That's the seal," said Callum. He was staring right at the wolf, face blank, eyes empty, but his hand was reaching for

Ziggy's again. "We still have to give it something. It wants a soul."

Ziggy stood up. In the gloom she looked into the wolf's yellow eyes. It was the creature from her painting brought to life, only somehow it was less frightening to her now than what it had represented when she drew it.

She unhooked the locket from her neck.

"Here's a piece of mine." She dropped the necklace onto the painting.

Lena turned around, tears on her face. She said nothing, but she quickly unfastened the leather strap of the watch on her wrist. She placed it on the painting.

Jamie was already clutching his Swiss Army Knife. Ziggy hadn't noticed he'd been carrying it, the blade already out, as if it might help against what was coming. He looked at it in his hand, smiled a little wryly, closed the blade, and dropped it onto the page.

Callum was crouched, his eyes trained on the creature, its muscles twitching with expectation, a low growl in the air smelling of rot and wet fur. He slipped the beaded bracelet from his wrist. He didn't place it with the others; he held it out to Ziggy. She took it carefully and put it down on the tree.

She folded the paper around them all, tucking the corners in tight, like a seed made of her childhood. She placed it in the hole, swallowing a breath so sharp it was painful. Together, the four of them pushed the earth; soft, heavy and wet, on top of it, covering it like a blanket.

The air had gone still. Ziggy looked up.

Through the darkness, she could see the crops parting like water. A huge shape moved towards the barbed wire fence, ethereal and grey, but somehow terrifyingly solid.

He sat atop a tar-black steed that snorted and pawed the earth. It stepped, not over the fence, but through it; ghostlike.

Lena made a choked noise in her throat.

The King of the Underworld smiled at them, eyes like blue fire, long hair whipping in the wind. He held the reins of the creature beneath him tight as a coiled spring and it danced in anticipation. When he spoke, it was in a voice softer than Ziggy could have imagined, like leaves on the wind. Words in a language she didn't understand, but she knew what he was saying.

Come. This is the end.

For a moment, as she pressed the dirt down, Ziggy panicked that she was wrong, that it wouldn't work. Perhaps, as she had always suspected, it would be easier to just let go. She saw a flash of the wolf's teeth, the smiling eyes of the antlered man.

Ink on paper, blood on grass.

The night seemed to pause, like the stars were holding their breath. Then the King of the Underworld lifted the horn to his lips. The sound rang out across the sky; and the creature stilled. It tilted its head, listening.

Then it turned, dropped its head and padded away on silent feet into the dark night.

Its master had already vanished. Gwyn Ap Nudd. Cernunnos. God or King, whoever he was. Ziggy didn't even see him disappear. The silence he left behind echoed. Even the wind had dropped, and nothing stirred in the hedges.

For a long moment, none of them moved. A bird took off out of a tree, flapping. Then Lena let out a trembling laugh; part disbelief, part grief, and sat down beside the mound of earth.

The others sat too. Jamie and Callum looked at each other,

and both started laughing. Muddy and breathless, blinking up at the sky. Ziggy smiled and breathed in the night air. The world felt tilted.

Jamie groaned. "I just remembered I've got an exam tomorrow."

And then, far off, a train rumbled past. Its high, ghostly whistle breaking through the stillness, a reminder that the world beyond the fields was still turning.

Epilogue

The August sun glinted off the windscreen of a passing ice-cream van. The tune it played was familiar to Ziggy, but she couldn't have named it. She turned to Lena, unable to keep the astonishment from her voice as it disappeared around the corner.

"Since when does that come around here?"

Lena blinked, open-mouthed.

"No way… We're on the map."

Ziggy laughed. They turned down the alley between the houses into the park, wondering aloud how much a Ninety-Nine cost these days, and then laughing some more at how old that made them sound.

"Ziggy's here, I'm not babysitting you anymore."

Luke puffed out his cheeks in exasperation as the girls approached the playground and mimed shooting himself in the head with a finger. Callum was on one of the swings, going back and forth at speed that suggested he was about to make an ill-advised jump.

"So?"

"BBC," Lena replied, grinning as widely as she had been all morning. "I'm dead chuffed. Must be a sign. BA in Journalism is calling me."

"Nice one," nodded Luke. "I'm just happy I didn't fail anything. What about you, *Da Vinci Code*?"

Ziggy felt her cheeks flush. Callum leapt from the swing, managed to land on his feet but rolled forward onto his knees and hands. Luke glanced back over his shoulder.

"Is he doing resits or what?" he asked under his breath.

Ziggy just shrugged. Lena put her arm around her and gave her a little squeeze.

"Ziggy smashed it, *obviously*. A in Art."

"Duh."

Callum came over, grinning like he was the one with exciting news. Ziggy had already texted him that morning with her exam results. It was so much less embarrassing that way. He pulled her into a bear hug without warning.

"Down boy," she murmured, but she was laughing.

"What did you want to show us?" Luke asked.

"I hope it's a pint at the pub," Lena suggested.

"That's what I said," Luke pulled a face. "But apparently somebody's boyfriend *still* isn't eighteen yet."

Callum smirked.

"Your mum would've known I'm a Leo."

Luke laughed at that.

"You're an actual Rugrat. Where's Jim-Jam?"

"Sulking over his D's," said Lena. "Come on, let's go get him."

The four of them strolled, lazy in the heat, back out towards the main road. Lena put on a pair of sunglasses and punched Luke in the arm when he said she looked like an Olsen twin. Struck by a whim, they nipped into the corner shop for ice lollies, Callum emptying his pockets of loose change, then walked more quickly to Jamie's house, dripping condensation.

"Your Calippo's melting," Ziggy thrust it into his hand at the door.

"I... thanks?"

"We're going for a walk," Callum blurted, nearly bouncing. Jamie looked at him flatly, then turned to Ziggy in mute appeal.

"Come on, you've got to see this," she smiled.

Lena had already pushed past him into the hall and was picking up his trainers and shouting lively greetings up the stairs to his mum. She dropped his shoes on the doorstep in front of him with a grin.

"You'd be so much prettier if you smiled more," she said.

Ziggy abruptly shoved Callum aside, not trusting him to hold back laughter. Thankfully he took the hint and turned his back, wandering off to stand on the pavement with Luke, his shoulders shaking slightly.

Jamie crouched to put on his shoes, but as he tipped his head, she thought she saw his mouth twitch, just a little.

They walked through the village, the streets quiet for a Thursday, a warm breeze shifting the leaves that were just about fading with the last colours of summer.

A woman was pushing an electric lawnmower across the grass outside Nana Peg's old bungalow. The rhododendrons had lost their blossoms, and bees circled the lavender, which spilled like a purple waterfall over the wall to the path. The woman raised a hand in greeting to Ziggy, and she smiled back. There was a soft ache in her chest, and she put her fingers to it, feeling for where the locket used to sit, and instead felt only her own heartbeat.

None of them really looked at the stump of the old apple tree as they crossed the train tracks. They were too busy playing keep away with Callum's lighter after Luke suggested he'd be able to afford a new bike by September if he'd stop smoking.

Ziggy replied to a text from Felicity, congratulating her on her results. She was going out to the beach on the train with some other friends this weekend and wondered if Ziggy wanted to come along. Ziggy replied that she had plans with her brother that evening, so she'd have to be back in time, but she'd love to go. She was already thinking about the cave, and the perspective she'd use to sketch it.

"Everyone else'll be sunbathing and flirting in bikinis and you'll be crouched on the rocks with a golf umbrella and a box of HB pencils," Luke joked.

"Sounds perfect," she grinned.

They walked along the dusty dirt path, watching a tractor harvest the field. A buzzard circled overhead, searching for mice disturbed from the crops. The ragwort swayed softly. Jamie and Callum argued about the new *Terminator* film.

At the flood bank, they climbed the fence. The grass was longer now. Jamie commented that the cows were nowhere in sight.

"They're around here somewhere," said Ziggy. "This field goes for miles, but they don't seem to like this end anymore." She saw Lena's back stiffen and reached for her. They walked along the ridge of the grassy bank, hand in hand.

"What are we looking for?" asked Luke. "I don't see anything."

"Up ahead," said Callum, a smile that barely contained his excitement. He kept taking quick paces as though he wanted to run ahead, but then hanging back again, letting Ziggy lead the way.

Lena was the first to see it.

"Shut the front door."

She dropped Ziggy's hand and rushed forwards. They all

hurried after her, Ziggy's pulse quickened.

The seedling stood a foot tall, reaching tentatively towards the sky. Delicate leaves, so pale they were almost white. Like paper. Its spindly stalk was a purplish brown. It quivered in the breeze. Lena crouched and reached out, hesitantly, to touch a leaf, as though checking it was solid. It wasn't like any tree that had ever grown before. Not in this world.

"It's real," she whispered.

Luke blinked in utter confusion. Jamie peered at it as though it was something from another planet. He took off his glasses and rubbed his eyes like he was in a movie. Callum stood back, fully entertained.

Even now, Ziggy sometimes still caught herself worrying that he was trying to trick her, and she hadn't quite believed it could be true, but here it was. Small and fragile, but vital. Budding with unformed promise.

"What if this one gets cut down?" Jamie asked in a small voice. "Or… I dunno, damaged in a storm. It's pretty exposed out here."

"Nah," said Callum, taking out his lighter again now they were all too distracted to stop him. "I reckon it's tougher than it looks. And anyway, we'll keep an eye on it, won't we?"

"Yes," agreed Lena firmly. She looked up at Ziggy with a fierce hope in her eyes. "And not just because it knows our names… because I want to."

Ziggy smiled. She crouched down next to Lena to look closer at the little plant, the midday sun warming the back of her neck.

Summer would soon be over, and then real life would begin again.

Author's Note

When I was about seventeen, some friends and I got scared by a dog in the middle of the night while inebriated near the Mill Pond next to the castle, in my hometown of Pembroke in West Wales. In hindsight it was really stupid, but we were convinced at the time that it wasn't a dog. Nowadays, the experience would be live on Tiktok and there'd be no living down the comments in the morning. I doubt the others who were there even remember the night that inspired this continuation of my stories from under the hill; but on the off chance that any of them are reading this... Dude. It was just a dog.

Everything that Jamie reads about Celtic Mythology in Chapter 20 is obviously based on real folklore. I personally always considered the wild hunt to be a feature of Norse mythology but found the connection to the Welsh king of the fair folk too tempting to pass up, and in the words of a friend of mine; "Fit. I totally would".

If you're curious about the Welsh folk tune that Ziggy's china shepherdess plays, it's called *Dacw NgharIad*. There's a beautiful version you can listen to on YouTube by Eve Goodman. Huge thanks to Angie James, whose social media and blog posts about the process of making natural inks and nature inspired art were absolutely fundamental to the creation of this story. Thank you to the wonderful community of readers and writers on Tiktok who have given me so much encouragement and friendship over the past year, I never expected to find so much love and support on the silly dance app. Thank you to my beta readers for their helpful and supportive feedback, to my mum who read it first, and most of all to Siân, who has been with me all the way, taught me what "syntax" means, and who insists I write Lena's story next.

About the Author

CT Klass has always been kind of spooky. She is originally from West Wales where she used to perform with local amateur theatrical groups and worked in a castle but moved to Yorkshire and started working in education, particularly with vulnerable children and those with additional needs. She enjoys books, films, theatre, pro-wrestling, rock music and rum. She lives with her husband, two children, her mother, some cats and a few ghosts. She's good value on Tiktok, if that's your thing.

Also by CT Klass

And No Birds Sing

He didn't recognise this creature stood in front of him. All the air in the room was gone.

"I'm hungry," she repeated, her voice soft and sweet. It made his skin crawl. "You don't look very tasty, but you'll have to do."

July 1999

Fourteen-year-old Nicky has been missing for eight months, and his friends still go out every day into the fields and farmland surrounding the village, to the place where they found his bloody Converse trainer floating in a stream. Something strange is lurking in hedgerows, a disturbing presence from the ancient English countryside, creeping into the lives of a group of teenagers. When Nicky's twin sister goes missing too, it begins a twisted chain of events that leaves their friends wondering who they can trust and just what evil is lurking in their quiet rural village.

And No Birds Sing is a sun-bleached, nostalgic, coming-of-age story in the tradition of British folk horror, perfect for 90's kids, weird kids, fans of *Stranger Things* and anyone who was ever scared to look out of their bedroom window at night but not sure why...

***

Wings

The theatre was swamped with a silence that felt heavy. It was not the anticipatory silence of a show about to start, but the dead silence of a show come to an end.

"By the pricking of my thumbs..." murmured January to herself.

The house doors are open at The Alexandra Theatre and the stage is set for a production of *A Midsummer Night's Dream*, but a there is a darkness backstage that has less to do with the fall of the curtains and more to do with the death of an actress the year before. Jasper works backstage in the theatre owned by his brother and is haunted by memories of Alice, the girl who died, and his own guilty conscience. When a face from the past returns and Jasper is plagued by disturbing visions, it becomes clear that he is not the only one haunted by The Alexandra's dark past and there is more than just his sanity at stake.

www.ingramcontent.com/pod-product-compliance
Lightning Source LLC
LaVergne TN
LVHW030920080826
845145LV00013B/2982

* 9 7 8 1 9 1 9 4 2 7 0 0 3 *